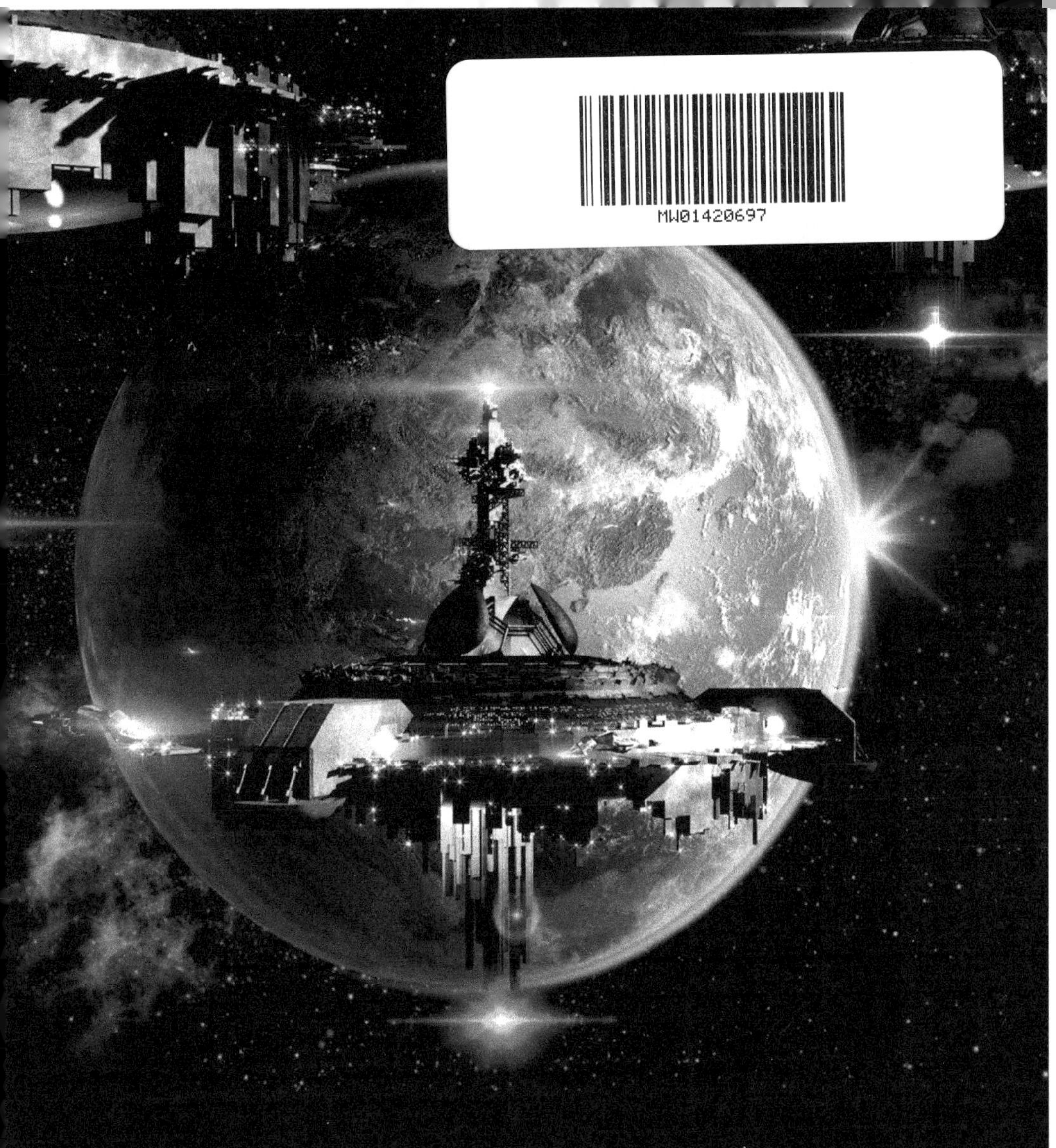

SEEKERS OF THE DOGAZOIDS

TIMOTHY NEWBREY

ARPress

Copyright © 2024 by Timothy Newbrey

All rights reserved. No part of this publication may be reproduced, distributed, or transmitted in any form or by any means, including, photocopying,recording, or other electronic or mechanical methods, without the prior written permission of the copyright owner and the publisher, except in the case of brief quotations embodied in critical reviews and certain other noncommercial uses permitted by copyright law. For permission requests, write to the publisher, addressed "Attention: Permissions Coordinator," at the address below.

ARPress
45 Dan Road Suite 5
Canton MA 02021
Hotline: 1(888) 821-0229
Fax: 1(508) 545-7580

Ordering Information:
Quantity sales. Special discounts are available on quantity purchases by corporations, associations, and others. For details, contact the publisher at the address above.

Printed in the United States of America.

ISBN-13:   Softcover   979-8-89330-763-4
            eBook   979-8-89300-764-1

Library of Congress Control Number: 2024903452

TABLE OF CONTENTS

CHAPTER 1 1

CHAPTER 2 26

CHAPTER 3 43

CHAPTER 4 57

CHAPTER 5 75

CHAPTER 6 86

CHAPTER 7 106

CHAPTER 8 118

ABOUT THE AUTHOR 142

For my mom Phyllis and my wife Sara. They both helped me through this adventure! I couldn't have done it without them.

And thanks to Girgio Tsoukalos and everyone at Ancient Aliens. I love your show! You're my inspiration.

CHAPTER 1

A LARGE SPACECRAFT IS TRANSPORTING beings from one planet (their home) to a new planet that has vast resources, enough to support their race. They are called the Anunnaki, and they come from the planet Nibiru. The planet's atmosphere is very polluted from years of mistreatment, including several nuclear wars. They had been a warring race of people in their past. Planetary conquest and dominance were key factors in these wars. Greed and lack of negotiation made it worse. The wars have left the planet barren. Space exploration has become a necessity for survival.

All the beings who live on Nibiru live inside the planet in subterranean dwellings and breathe filtered air. This is necessary due to the outside atmosphere being so polluted. But life goes on. The Anunnaki are very intelligent beings. They are superb space travelers, and with this knowledge, they plan to save their race from its destructive past and move on to a better future. Starting with a new planet, they plan to live in peace!

The Anunnaki, whose appearance is reptilian or humanoid in their original form, are also masterful shape-shifters, which means they can change their appearance. They can change into human form. They can also alter their state to become large intimidating creatures. Some can morph into animal form too. It's a gift they have had over the centuries, the ability to change form. But it doesn't get used much in this day and age. Now that the wars are over, it becomes less important to change into something else. But the ability to do so is still there. Shape-shifting is sometimes used for manual labor (large beings) or for entertainment. But its usefulness elsewhere is limited.

The planet Nibiru has been relatively peaceful since the last devastating war. And several generations have passed. Time has healed some of the wounds of war. Although the warring countries have made peace, the damage to the planet's atmosphere is irreparable. This has been recognized, and space exploration has been successful enough that they have found a compatible planet to relocate to. So they can save their race, vowing to live in peace and not make the same mistakes of the past.

Back onboard the large spacecraft, called the V-34, everything is quiet. It is the sleeping hours for the passengers. A small crew of three officers are flying the craft as it floats silently through space, another successful run, bringing beings to the new planet. The missions are becoming more routine.

The vessel is large enough to carry two hundred passengers comfortably. They are mostly set up in family quarters, but there are single adults also. The ship has a nice cafeteria and a big recreation room to ease the passengers' minds on long voyages.

These ships are large and circular, about fifty yards in diameter, and silver or chrome in color. They are an impressive sight, though not made for war. They are a peaceful craft, built for transport.

In the beginning of the evacuation process, there were ships that were leftovers from wartime being used for transport. They were stripped of their weapons and for the most part were old and rickety, having been fired upon, damaged, and then repaired. They were questionable to say the least.

The ship's name, the V-34, has meaning. The "V" stands for Vimana, which was an ancient flying craft or saucer (no really!). The number 34 signifies it being the thirty-fourth one built. The next one is almost finished, thusly named the V-35. As they are completed, each one is improved slightly over the previous model. The beat goes on.

So at first, the evacuation was not very successful. Two of the aging warships were lost in meteor showers they couldn't avoid or outrun. Both were filled with passengers. All perished. After the second disaster, a decision was made to build new ships. It took a little time to get organized and a little more time to build the facility for manufacturing new transport vehicles. But they did it. The Anunnaki are persistent and intelligent beings. And if survival of their race meant building new crafts to fly out of Nibiru, they could do it. Why not? They built all the warships that caused this mass evacuation. Nice going, right? Now it's time to fly the bleep out.

So now things are going well. Thirty-five of the new vessels have been built. The old warships were melted down and used to build the new ones, no waste incurred. These aliens really know their stuff when it comes to building spaceships. They've been doing it for centuries.

Onboard the V-34, Commander Zilog (the head guy) is just waking from his sleep. He joins the three officers at the helm of the ship. They exchange pleasantries, and the officers inform the chief how the flight has been while he slept. There were no meteor showers or other obstructions in space, although all in charge are anxious to try the ship's upgraded acceleration, but only in the event of problems. Supposedly this bad boy has a better intake system that creates much more low-end torque, which improves power "off the line" so to speak. But not yet it doesn't, not until there's an emergency.

Commander Zilog (let's go back to him) is an older man, a military lifer. He has been flying these big saucers for years, and he knows them well. He has also had many close calls in them. He got shot down during the first war and was lucky to survive. Next, he flew battered warships in the second war, another very dangerous assignment. And now he has a safe, pleasant job—transporting his passengers to the new planet, a peaceful assignment. Nobody is shooting at him. Zilog loves it. It seems hard for him to imagine flying around peacefully. But this is his fourth trip to the new planet, and nobody is shooting at him.

So the poor guy has been through hell early in his military career. It's only right that he gets one of these gravy jobs flying transports.

And even better, he's in a brand-new vessel this time out. This is the V-34's maiden voyage. Zilog was proud to be part of the ceremony when they launched her. It was a grand time, a lot of hoopla, cheering, confetti, and stuff like that. Not really Zilog's bag, he's a more quiet kind of guy. But he suffered through the celebration like a good soldier does. And now he has the honor of flying this brand-new ship. He can't help feeling unworthy of this honor. Zilog lost a number of dear friends in the two ships that were lost, and he thinks of them often, as though they are right there with him. He's in his new ship, and he feels his lost friends all around him.

Anyway, as he sits down in his commander's seat, TV monitors around the bridge begin to come on showing areas of the ship where passengers are beginning to stir. Everything is peaceful as people come to the cafeteria for their first meal.

The meals on board are created by what's called a manna machine. It makes food out of almost any raw material. The food is bland, but it sustains life. The passengers are okay with it, because they are all happy to be on this transport leaving their doomed planet. So the manna food is okay, whether it looks like green mush or not.

The manna machine itself is large and complicated, but several crewmembers are specially trained on disassembly and cleaning. So as long as they keep this machine maintained, it will provide food for them.

The cafeteria is a place to congregate. People gossip and chat as they eat. Zilog sees this on one monitor and decides to go and visit and also make a round of his ship. He gets up out of his control chair and says bye to his officers. He heads out of the control room and down a corridor. As he walks, he is thinking pleasantly of these trips to the new planet, helping his race. He feels good about it, transporting people in peacetime. He's so weary of the fighting that this assignment is a blessing. Friendly faces are all around—no more enemies and no more near-death situations. He snaps himself out of a mini flashback as he walks into the main propulsion room, the first stop on his round of the ship. Zilog is proud of the engine components this beast has. He picked a lot of them himself. He's an expert with these propulsion systems. And he's good friends with the boys who put them together back on Nibiru. They built him a speedy one this time. As he strolls around this magnificent new machine, Zilog takes a feeling of pride knowing that his people built it.

Zilog is approached by his nephew, Kornak, and they stand together admiring the ship's propulsion system. Kornak is Zilog's sister's boy. Their relationship hasn't been that good, sort of rocky so to speak. But young Kornak has cleaned up his act recently. He joined the military and turned away from his previous rather "seedy" lifestyle. Zilog was impressed with seeing Kornak's changing ways. He was happy to see the boy doing better for himself, so much so that he relented to his sister's wishes and brought Kornak along on this voyage. It was a risk. Zilog realized this, but he felt like he had to do it, because he loves his sister. And he's willing to give the boy another shot. So all is well between them. Kornak has reached a good rank during his time in the military. He's a corporal, and he also knows these ships fairly well, not as well as his uncle though. But at least it gives them something to chat about when the conversation lulls. Neither of them care to talk about old times. That's for sure.

So as they stroll through the engine room chatting, Kornak assures Zilog that all is well. Next, they move into the adjoining room where the fuel cells are located. This ship, as with others in the fleet, is powered by a mixture of three fuels that arrive simultaneously in the pressurized manifold. Two of the fuel ingredients are in larger amounts than the third. But the third one is very important even though it's a much smaller amount in the mixture. It is extremely important for combustion.

The two larger fuel tanks are first in the room, and Zilog checks their gauges as they pass. Both are fine, about three quarters full, right where they're supposed to be.

But as he comes to the third tank, he sees that its gauge is showing extremely low, almost empty. This startles Zilog very much, and he becomes angry immediately. He has a reputation for angry outbursts. His lizard-like face takes on an expression of anger. He turns to Kornak; and in a low growling voice, he asks, "Is this gauge malfunctioning?"

Kornak, looking surprised and frightened, responds, "It shouldn't be, sir."

Zilog, now in a much louder voice, says, "Well then why does it say it's empty? Weren't these tanks filled before we left port?"

Kornak, now stuttering a little with fear, says, "The guys at the assembly p-p-plant told me that everything was ready to go!"

Zilog, still yelling, replies, "And you didn't check it?!"

Kornak now almost crying says, "They said it was done. I was getting my stuff together for the trip. I thought everything was taken care of, sir!"

Zilog now furious storms out of the propulsion room yelling things that are unintelligible. He's very angry. As he gets back to the control area, where he left his three crewmen just a few minutes ago, his mood is not good. And as he is telling his crew (loudly) about the low fuel crisis, the alarm sounds for low fuel. Lights are flashing around the room. Zilog is boiling mad.

He screams to no one in particular, "We've got to land this thing somewhere! When that alarm starts, we've got twenty-five minutes till it runs all the way empty. Then we drift in space or crash into some planet to our deaths! Damn it! Why did I bring him on board?" He walks quickly to a map of planets and stars that they pass on their voyage. He's never had to do this before. The other trips have gone smoothly for the most part. There was never any fuel problems. All ships had been fueled properly—not this time.

But no matter what the cause, Zilog has an emergency on his hands, and he has to step up to save the lives of everyone on board. He sees the nearest planet to their location is a small world called Earth. Zilog had heard of it but had never been there. He knew that Earth was a warring planet, and his people had not gone there for this reason. Nevertheless, he points his ship at it and hopes to God he has enough fuel to reach it. A crash landing means death for all on board.

If this thing were to run out of fuel, it would drop out of the sky like a stone.

Zilog is trying his best to hold his temper, although his forehead is sweating and his hands are trembling slightly. He skillfully controls the machine as it comes into Earth's atmosphere. The other crewmembers watch with worried faces. He reduces speed to near idle to conserve fuel and looks to the planet below to find land, a continent. He can't land this thing in the water. So he maneuvers the big craft until he is over land and begins final descent.

The passengers onboard are frightened by this sudden emergency landing. They are gathered in the rec or dining area and are worried about what the heck is going on. Babies are crying as a murmur falls over the crowd. Zilog is monitoring the situation, seeing them getting worried. While he lands his ship, he instructs one crewmember to turn on the "calming mist." This new system flows to the different rooms of the ship, calming everyone in there. It looks to be working just fine. Everyone is quickly calming as Zilog can see on his monitor. So he looks to another monitor to find a spot to land his ship. He finds one that looks suitable, no obstructions, just green grass (somewhere in rural Virginia). Zilog sees it, he likes it, and he sets his ship down perfectly—a very nice landing for such a rushed panic. Commander and crew performed excellently, with a few minutes' worth of fuel to spare too. All are safe. Thank goodness for that.

Zilog uses another new feature this ship has. It's an electronically created screen that looks like woods and brush to conceal the ship outside, very impressive. Other screens are available too, besides woods. One is a rocky hillside with a pretty stream running down it. Anyway, he picked the woodsy one, because it looks natural in this field. And it hides the ship well.

So now let's take a moment from the story and meet the members of Zilog's crew. You've already met Kornak. Although he's in trouble right now, he's still a good kid. Now how about the rest of this brave crew? There are four members who monitor the power components of the vessel. They are essential on every voyage. They are Mezruh, Orsello, Beltran, and of course Kornak. These crewmembers have been trained on the ship's propulsion system and all related aspects. Three of the four are middle-aged veterans, and all take their jobs very seriously. The fourth is Kornak. He's new, and he's never been on one of these flights before. His military career thus far has been mostly mechanical, working on these new vessels. Also there are three more members of the crew to introduce. They are assigned to help fly the ship, help with the passengers, and keep the manna machine maintained. Their names are Melomar and Troxler (two men) and Adria (one woman). These three are very close-knit. They've flown together for some time now for two previous commanders. Zilog picked them after reviewing their backgrounds and acts of heroism. He liked that they had been together so long—a well-proven crew of veterans. Zilog met them for the first time at the big V-34 launch party yesterday.

Melomar, Troxler, Adria, I've got to remember those names, Zilog thought.

So here they are, stranded on a hostile planet. The big question now is what to do next. They need the element of fuel that is essential to power their craft. It is a vaporized substance made from what we Earth people call gold! That's right! Gold is what they need to power their craft. But they have to find some. They have the machine that vaporizes it. So that's not a problem. They just got to get some. Zilog summons his crewmembers to the control room. He has a plan. This is a first for everyone. Landing on a strange hostile planet? Nope, not one of them has ever done this before.

As the four absent crewmembers come through the entry door, the mood is tense. All are present, eight lizard people with uniforms on. All of them are very serious looking. No one is laughing or kidding around. This is a life-or-death situation that must be resolved.

Zilog brings them to order by raising his hand and saying, "Attention, everyone. As you all know, we have a problem." Without casting any blame he pauses, while everyone glances angrily at Kornak. They all know he's to blame here. Word travels fast on this thing. Zilog continues, "We have a fuel shortage."

Mezruh asks respectfully, "Why wasn't it filled in port, sir?"

The commander responds, "Apparently, it was overlooked in the excitement." Kornak looks down at the floor, again with the angry looks from everyone. Zilog goes on, "But we have to move on. We'll get through this. I've got something planned."

Zilog plays the role of leader so well. He is confident when he speaks, and he never shows weakness. His listeners feel assured of his leadership. He goes on speaking, "We're on this planet temporarily. It is called Earth. It is a hostile planet. We don't know much about it, but we do know that these beings are war mongers, so we need to stay away from them. Our quest is for gold, so I plan to send out a two-person exploration unit to see what will be needed to obtain some. We're not sure what's out there. But we are a brave and strong race (he raises his fist), and we'll get what we need to continue this mission!" He lowers his fist, looking around sternly at his comrades. Then he continues speaking, "I'll need two volunteers. Who wants to go explore this planet?"

Everyone responds excitedly with yes. They all want to go. And even if deep inside they don't, it doesn't matter. They are trained to be fearless. It is a proud moment for Commander Zilog. There is no fear in this room! All seven of his officers are willing to put themselves in harm's way for this cause (seeking gold).

He chooses two—Mezruh and Orsello. They look to be good choices—big and strong, intelligent and serious, and brave of course. Zilog singles them out a bit and begins briefing them while the others listen. He says, "I'll need you two to shape-shift to human form. You'll fit in fine when you look similar to this race. Try to have as little contact as possible. These beings are dangerous, so just try to find where the gold is as discreetly as possible. Then return with your findings, and we'll go from there." He then looks around to the rest of the group and goes on speaking, "I'll also need anyone who leaves this ship, for any reason, to shift to human form. We don't need these beings seeing us in this reptilian look. It might scare them too much."

Orsello adds, in his low voice, "Yeah, we're pretty scary, aren't we, sir?" All chuckle a bit, and the mood lightens up some, except for Kornak. He's being quiet. He feels like an outcast, a stranger in the crowd.

Zilog begins speaking again. He's ending the meeting. "So attention, everyone. Let's return to our stations, except you two." He points to Mezruh and Orsello. "I've got some more instructions for you." As the others file out the door, he begins speaking to his boys, "Now listen, guys. We've got to be very careful out there. When we come upon the gold we seek, we can't take it forcefully. We are peaceful. And of course, we have no weapons." The guys agree by nodding their heads and continue listening intently. Zilog goes on, "So take the utility vehicle. It will need to be unloaded in the cargo bay first and go explore. Of course, you'll need human form but nothing crazy, no big muscles or anything else distracting, just regular humans. Take the truck until you start to see some civilization. Then hide our truck, and hopefully you can . . . ahem . . . borrow something from this planet to ride around in." Mezruh and Orsello glance at each other with worried looks as the commander talks. "We don't want to show our truck to anyone here. That would tip 'em off for sure!"

Mezruh pipes up, "Yeah, I bet they don't have anything like that around here."

Zilog agrees, but then he changes the subject. He asks them how well or if at all can they read this language. He says, "I know we all speak it, but not all of us can read it." It wasn't a required course because it wasn't the primary language on Nibiru. It's not even called English. Anyway, as it turns out, Mezruh is somewhat capable of reading this language, but Orsello is not. "One out of two will do just fine," Zilog says with a smile. "Just remember to stay together. Stay low key. Don't attract any attention." Both men agree. They're going to try their hand at being spies, sort of. Zilog tells them, "You guys will leave in the morning's first light. Do your shape-shifting then and put on some average-looking clothes. We're not sure yet how these people dress, so let's just look bland, somewhere in the middle." The men agree and assume that the meeting is almost over. But Zilog has a little more. "Oh, yes, one more thing, gentlemen. Go ahead and unload the utility vehicle tonight so it'll be ready to go in the morning. Grab a couple of the passengers to help you. It'll be fun you'll see," he says jokingly. Mezruh and Orsello chuckle and give him a hearty "Yes, sir!" as they head out. They're officially on a mission. Both are excited about it. They walk down the corridor toward the rec area. They hear sounds that sound like a party going on. Mezruh opens the door, and sure enough there is a party in there. Everyone looks very content, talking, laughing, and such. Kids are running around. The calming mist seems to be working just marvelous. These lizard-looking people have to quiet down to hear what the two have to say. Mezruh raises his hand to speak (like he saw Zilog do a little while ago), "Hi, everybody, um . . . I need a couple of volunteers." (He's not a good speaker like Zilog.) He goes on, "I need two men to help me and my buddy" (he points his thumb at Orsello who waves awkwardly at the crowd). Mezruh continues, "We've got some work to do in the cargo area."

Two men step forward as soon as he is done speaking. "Right here, sir!" says one guy looking eager.

The other dude is happy too. "Ready to work, sir!" he exclaims while flexing his muscles.

They are both very cheerful. Maybe it's the calming mist doing its job. Ya think? So Mezruh instructs these two gentlemen to return to their quarters, morph into something giant, and meet them at the cargo area. The reason they go back to quarters is to save their clothes from being torn up, when they morph into giants. They (the Anunnaki) have learned about shape-shifting to something big with your clothes on ruins your clothes! In addition, you don't do it in front of females and offspring, just for manners.

Anyhow, getting back to the story, the two volunteers turn and head across the room toward their quarters to change so to speak. Mezruh and his buddy Orsello say goodbye to the few people who are still listening. They head out the doors they just came through, as people go back to chatting. All seem to be calm. No one thought to ask about the emergency landing. They're all good.

So the guys (M and O) head down the hallway to the cargo area, where they take off their uniforms, neatly mind you, and fold them. The military people wear elastic-style shorts that allow for expansion upon shape-shifting. They look like basketball shorts from the 1980s. It's kind of dorky by our standards, but they like 'em. And they expand to a much bigger size, which is what happens now as the guys get this serious look on their faces and morph into much larger beings, muscular intimidating creatures, monsters sort of, by our standards anyway—lizard-like giants, very creepy, about nine feet tall, humanoid of course but huge. After their transformation, the two move to the rear of the utility vehicle and open the doors. It is a box-style truck, loaded to the max with supplies and food, including raw material for the manna machine.

And what do you know? Here come the other two guys who are gonna help. They too have morphed into a giant form as instructed. They too have elastic shorts on. They all look ridiculous (by our standards)—four giant lizard-like men wearing basketball shorts. Looking good, boys!

They talk cheerfully as the unloading gets under way. Mezruh starts telling how nice the new planet is and how lucky they are to have found it. One of the guys helping asks him, "So is this it? Are we at our new home?"

Mezruh thinks a moment and comes back with, "No, this is . . . um . . . a maintenance stop. You know, check all the fluid levels and make sure everything is alright." He's lying of course. He doesn't want these guys to know what's really going on. So he told them a weak lie.

Next question, "Why are we unloading this truck?" asks the other helper.

Orsello takes this one. "Because um . . ." he starts. "Well, because we're leaving it here. These guys need it." He glances at Mezruh as he speaks, to see if his buddy has anything to add. He doesn't. So Orsello goes a little further with his fake story. He's starting to have some fun with it now. "Yeah, they asked if they could have this one because theirs blew up!" All of them laugh although the two volunteers aren't sure why.

Just then, as the four are laughing and talking, Kornak walks up, hoping to join in. But they all get quiet instead. Mezruh and Orsello are mad at him and the other two guys can see that, but they don't know why. Kornak asks Mezruh, "Do you guys need any more help doing this?"

Mezruh responds quickly and with anger, "No, we don't. We've got this." Kornak begins to speak again, but Mezruh interrupts him speaking louder now, "We don't need your help. You've done enough, haven't you?" He looks angrier now. The others look away and continue working. The two volunteer dudes are wondering what is going on here. They came to help, which they are, but now these military guys are getting mad at each other. The vols are eating it up. What gossip this will be when they get back to the cafeteria. So Mezruh continues with his little rant, "You think you can just jump in anywhere and just . . ." His thoughts begin to waver a bit. He waves his hand toward the exit and says loudly, "Why don't you go do the bathrooms or something?" Orsello chuckles a little at this suggestion, and that causes the others to laugh too as Kornak walks away dejected. Mezruh is still looking at him with much anger on his face. The other two guys can only wonder what Kornak did to draw such anger from him.

Meanwhile, back in the main control room, Zilog is seated in his captain's chair. He's looking at one of his monitors that shows the history of this planet. It tells mostly about the wars we've had and how violent our history has been. There's nothing about gold though. *Hmm . . .* he thinks, *not much help at all. This planet is considered to be a very hostile place. That's why only limited research has ever been done here.* He knows there is gold here somewhere, but he doesn't know where. So when he sends his guys out in the morning, they will be starting cold, and that worries Zilog very much. He just met these men. He surely doesn't want to lose them because of this. In the back of his mind, he pictures himself strangling his nephew. *I should have never brought him on board this ship*, he thinks. *Now look at us, stranded on some strange hostile planet. Two hundred and seven lives are at stake, because of one fool.* He still can't believe it. But he continues searching for information on this god-forsaken planet, his mind crowded with anger.

Back in the cargo bay, things are going well. The four giants are working up a sweat, talking pleasantly as they unload. Most of the products they're working with are dried foods, farm tools, seeds to plant for crops, and harvested crops to be used by the manna machine. All very important items are stacked semi-neatly. Soon the unloading is complete, and all that is left to do is to unshackle the truck from the floor. Mezruh goes over to one of the many tool boxes and gets out two large wrenches for the job. There are four turnbuckles holding the truck to the floor.

And after a few minutes of wrenching by Mezruh and Orsello, the job is done! Turnbuckles are loosened and removed, and this big truck is ready for some exploration—but not till tomorrow though, first thing.

Mezruh dismisses the two volunteers, thanking them of course for their help. As they head out of the cargo area, they both shape-shift back to normal size, two average-size guys with big baggy shorts on. They got this shape-shifting stuff down. No clothes get ruined or anything. Imagine the savings.

So our two heroes go ahead and morph down too. They also look like little guys in big shorts. But their shorts match, military uniform-style. They look cool, but baggy.

Commander Zilog comes walking down the corridor and into the cargo area.

He sees his men resting and chatting a bit. As he walks up to them, he is very impressed with all the hard work they have done. He tells them cheerfully, "You guys are awesome! Got it unloaded fast, and it's all stacked out of the way too! Beautiful!" He waves his arms around as he talks. He's a very expressive guy. And he's liking the scene here. *It's nice*, he thinks, *that I can trust these two men to do good work*, unlike someone else he can think of. He clenches his fist as a pleasant thought turns into an angry one, but only for a moment. He turns to Orsello and says, "Let's take a look outside."

This is very exciting for all three, as their faces all kind of light up. They look around at each other. "Let's go!" Mezruh says with excitement. No fear! They haven't explored this atmosphere at all, although their environmental monitors say it's okay. All three guys are pumped for this. Mezruh heads for the control panel that opens the door. Zilog and Orsello are waiting impatiently. Mezruh calls out to them, his voice echoes in this cavernous room they are in, "It looks like it's warm and sunny, sir. Ninety degrees."

Zilog answers back, "Sounds good. Open the door."

Orsello repeats it but louder in his gravel-sounding voice, "Open the door, Mezruh!" They both giggle a bit as Mezruh hits the button. And down goes the immense door.

It turns into a ramp as it hits the ground outside. Daylight comes flooding in. "Sweet daylight!" Zilog exclaims loudly as it gleams across him and Orsello. Then Mezruh steps into it from the shadow he had been behind. He too is amazed by the sunlight. Now all three are enjoying this moment. None of them have seen it a long time. There is no "sunshine" on their home planet Nibiru, just clouds and overcast all the time—yucky-looking grayish-red clouds and a cold biting wind too, toxic wind, full of nuclear by-products. It's just a really nasty atmosphere overall. It's no wonder they're all leaving. The place is falling apart.

So our three heroes bask in the sun for a few more moments. Two are still in their baggy gym shorts, looking kind of silly. But that's okay. They are having fun. The mood is light, for now.

Zilog walks over to the control panel that opens the door. It has the intercom system also.

He pushes a button and speaks to the panel, "All crewmembers report to the cargo area."

As he does this, Mezruh and Orsello head over to their clothes and start putting them on.

Zilog steps back into the sunshine to wait for the rest of his crew.

And here they come now.

He wants them to see this! Even if they are on some hostile planet, most of his crew hasn't seen a nice atmosphere like this. Even if the trees they're looking at are not real, it's still a nice day!

So here they are all eight of them, standing on the ramp enjoying the sunshine, marveling at the blue sky with its white clouds moving by and the green grass on the ground. We Earth people take all this for granted. Blue sky, big whoop. But if you've never seen it, it's truly a thing of beauty. They are amazed by it.

As they stand there chatting (eight lizard people in uniforms), Mezruh approaches Zilog with a question, "Commander, shall I bring out the utility vehicle?" he asks. "We got it unloaded pretty fast."

Zilog agrees saying, "Sounds like a good idea, Mezruh. Go do some exploring maybe." Orsello is listening in looking excited. He is eager to go too. So Zilog is okay about the two going out for a while, saying, "It looks like we'll have light from their sun for a while, so go. But remember what we discussed." He puts one hand on Mezruh's shoulder and the other on Orsello's as he speaks, "I want you two to be super careful out there. Morph to humans of course, but nothing flamboyant! Just average-looking guys, okay?" He looks at both of them very seriously as they nod their heads yes. Zilog goes on, "And remember: When you start coming around some civilization, ditch this thing (he points at the utility vehicle) and drive something from around here, so you blend in."

So the two guys turn and head back up the ramp toward the truck. Zilog has a little more instructions for them as they walk away. He speaks in a louder voice since they are further away, "And remember, guys, we can't use any force or aggressive behavior. Keep to yourselves. Don't mingle with this dangerous race. Just check things out." By now Mezruh and Orsello have stopped walking to receive Zilog's instructions (again). The other crewmembers are listening too as Zilog goes on, "See if you can find us some gold. I have faith in you. Be careful." The other officers on the ramp begin cheering them on too, as they turn and walk past all the unloaded cargo.

Mezruh suddenly remembers something and slaps Orsello on the arm. "We forgot our street clothes!" he says.

They both stop and look at each other. Then they turn toward the corridor that leads to their quarters and take off in a jog. Mezruh yells over to Zilog, "Got to get our clothes, sir."

"Plain stuff, you guys," Zilog yells back with a smile. "Get out of those uniforms!" he says. Then he turns to his officers for some more chatting. It's very enjoyable for them all to be in this wonderful atmosphere, even though danger looms. They have forgotten for a moment that they are on a hostile planet and their futures are in doubt. They surely don't know what to expect from the beings who occupy this planet. Zilog relies on his military training and experience to tell him to expect the worst. Then maybe it might not be as bad as he had anticipated, hopefully. Maybe this race has compassion and sympathy. Wouldn't that be great?

As he is thinking these thoughts, he is interrupted by Adria standing next to him on the ramp. She asks, "Is our new planet as nice as this one seems to be, sir?"

"It is indeed," Zilog responds, speaking softly. "If only we were there now."

Adria has a question to ask her commander, but she hesitates. She's kind of scared to ask it.

Then the moment is lost as Beltran steps up to them and begins talking. He says, "This sure is a nice place. Too bad it's already taken" (the planet he means).

Zilog responds with, "It would be nice, but we're just visiting. Besides, Beltran (Zilog remembered his name), we don't know these humans very well. They might not like us." Everyone chuckles a little as Kornak steps into the conversation circle. Zilog continues, "If we can just camp out here for a few days until we get our situation corrected (he glares at Kornak briefly as Kornak stares down at the ramp) and then we'll be on our way." The anger is apparent in Zilog's voice as he finishes speaking. Seeing Kornak rekindled the flame. Zilog doesn't want to talk anymore. So he gathers everyone with an arm gesture, and speaking in a gentle voice he says, "I wanted you all to see the beauty here and know that our new home is similar to this planet." He pauses and looks around at them. He has a serious and concerned look on his face. Then he speaks again, "And I'm going to get us there!"

All cheer him on as he finishes. "We know you will, sir!" Just then the utility vehicle fires up behind them startling everyone a bit. They move to one side of the ramp as it approaches.

It looks like a futuristic army truck, streamlined and aerodynamic. And our heroes are looking good too. They got their plain guy clothes on. Both have shifted into middle-aged-looking humans.

Everything is on track. Zilog jumps up on the running board to wish them luck and give some last-minute instructions. He tells them, "Now don't stay gone long. Don't mingle with these dangerous beings. Just see what you can find out." He looks down at their clothes and complements them by saying, "Your outfits look good too. All is in order. You two be good out there."

And with that Zilog jumps down from the running board and rejoins his officers standing in the grass at the bottom of the ramp. Mezruh backs the big truck down the ramp and does a three-point turn. With the other officers cheering and clapping, the truck disappears into the imaginary trees. Who knows what'll happen next.

Zilog dismisses his officers to their duties, and they all walk up the ramp talking pleasantly as they go. He stops at the panel that closes the door and does so (closes the door). He can't risk the passengers seeing the beautiful climate here. They might scatter and never come back.

Besides, they are happy where they are for now—in the cafeteria, chillin'.

And Adria never got to ask the captain what she wanted to ask him. She missed the opportunity. But she's not done. You'll see.

Zilog returns to the control room to see what else he can do about their situation. He needs to try to contact the home planet and let them know of this flight's misfortune. Communication is almost impossible when the ship is in a different solar system from their own. He tries to send several messages but gets no response. So he gives up on that for now.

He then brings up the few files he has on planet Earth. He needs to review the ways of this race. How wild, he thinks, that he is trapped on some planet he barely knows, with no fuel in his brand- new ship! His fists clench as he reminds himself what caused it— sabotaged by stupidity.

But anyway, back to what he was doing, he is researching human behavior. *Hmmm*, he thinks as he scans the limited information he has. *Wars, wars, and more wars, these beings are a lot like us in our distant past—germ warfare, huge loss of life, nuclear bombs.* Zilog is scared to death reading this. He's not seeing anything good about this place at all. He hopes his boys will be okay.

As Mezruh and Orsello head out in the utility vehicle, their heads are filled with question marks. How far do they have to go until they find civilized beings? What will happen then?

How do these beings keep their gold? And where is it? (There are a lot of question marks.)

They come upon the country road that is nearby their ship. Mezruh says, "Let's get on this and see where it goes."

Orsello agrees saying, "It must be here for a reason. I'd say it'll lead us to some kind of community." So off they go in their big truck trying to look inconspicuous. They both look human, so they blend in, except for this futuristic machine they're driving. They can't shape-shift this thing!

Soon they come upon a town, a small town. So as instructed by their commander, they pull their truck into a woodsy area and leave it. Now they are on foot, just a couple of humans walking along, very normal-looking. They talk casually as they walk.

Orsello says, "Man, what a crazy voyage this is turning into."

Mezruh replies, "I know! Some dumb new guy forgot to fuel the ship! And he's the commander's nephew! Zilog is mad at him!"

"That kid might not get another shot at flying these missions."

"That's if we live through this one."

Orsello responds to Mezruh, "Don't think like that, Mezruh! Stay positive. We just got to explore a bit and find the magic elixir. We're smarter than these beings. Just don't make any of them mad or let them find out who we really are, and we won't get killed."

"I know. I was just kidding. I'm not scared. But this is all happening so fast."

"Oh, I know it! Here we are doing this (he waves his arms up). This isn't our regular job, you know?"

Mezruh agrees, "I know, buddy. I know."

As they walk they come upon their first brush with human activity. It's a feedstore with several cars parked in front. As they watch, another car pulls up and stops, and two humans get out.

The humans go into the feedstore, so Mezruh and Orsello approach the vehicle. The door has been left unlocked. Looking not very stealthy because neither one of them has ever done this before, they jump in. Mezruh is on the driver's side where all the controls are. He takes a deep breath and exhales heavily. He looks around at all the gadgets and is perplexed at what makes this thing start and run. It is very different from their truck. That's for sure.

Suddenly two humans, a woman and a child, come out of the feedstore. The woman is carrying a big bag (potatoes). Mezruh and Orsello are frozen with fear as the two humans walk up to the car next to the one they are trying to make off with. Mezruh watches as the woman puts her big bag into the back seat of the car. The child gets in on the passenger side. Trying not to stare, but very interested in how she's gonna make that thing move, they glance over and watch but look away quickly as she holds a clump of shiny objects (keys) up to the steering column. Then they hear the engine start, and she reaches for what looks like a stick (shifter) and moves it. The vehicle begins to move backward and then forward as it gets near the road and is gone.

Mezruh says out loud, "How hard can this be?" He looks down at the steering column. He sees the ignition where he saw the human put something in, and he begins shape-shifting his fingers to fit it. He then turns his hand (like he just saw). And vroom it starts! They are elated!

"Whoo-hoo!" Orsello proclaims. "Let's go!"

Mezruh next tries the stick thingy like he saw and boom! The car starts going backward. He has his hands on the wheel, but he hasn't noticed the gas and brake pedal yet. So the car goes backward into the road. It goes across the road and into the ditch on the other side before Mezruh can figure out how to make it go forward. (He still hasn't.) Now the car is slightly stuck. Then wouldn't you know it, here come the guys who just got out of it. They are both carrying bags. As they turn to where their car had been, they see that it isn't there anymore. A quick visual scan of the area and they see their car in the ditch on the other side of the road, with two hooligans trying to steal it. Just then Mezruh (now panicking) sees the pedals on the floor. Their truck doesn't have this crap! He mashes one with his foot, but nothing happens. The humans are approaching rapidly. Both have thrown their bags to the ground, and they look mad. So he mashes the other pedal, and the vehicle springs to life, still in reverse mind you. Our boys panic, and fear turns back to elation as the car shoots backward across a field, dust flying.

The two humans slow their run to a walk as they wonder what these two thieves are trying to pull. "Steal a car in reverse? What the hell?"

Inside the car, our heroes are happy to be moving away from the angry humans. But they're still unable to get it to go forward. So they quickly decide to abandon ship, as a group of humans are gathering outside the feedstore pointing at them. Into the woods they go, leaving the car there—doors open and engine running, still in reverse. No key is in the ignition.

Back on the V-34, Zilog has summoned the remainder of the crew (Kornak included) to the control room so he can share what information he has compiled on this planet.

As his officers enter the room, Zilog welcomes them and begins speaking, "I've got what information I could gather on this planet, and I'll be honest there isn't much. This planet hasn't been researched or even approached for decades because of its status as a warring planet. It has been bypassed." And then he goes on, "There are good people here. There are charitable organizations, which help those in need. But this planet has had many warring countries, bitter adversaries that caused mass destruction. The last ones we have here on record are called . . . um . . . Germany and Japan." He hopes he pronounced them right.

Everyone tries their best to look interested, out of respect for their commander. Adria suppresses a yawn as Zilog goes on talking, "Apparently these two countries joined forces and tried to take control of the rest of the planet. But the other major forces on the planet . . . let's see. It says here . . . America, England, and Russia. All joined forces and, after a long and destructive war, defeated . . . um . . . uh . . . oh yes, Germany and Japan. In one case here—no wait, two times—atomic force was used to subdue the aggressor." He pauses again and looks very concerned at his officers and goes on, "What I'm saying here is that this race is dangerous and we don't want anything to do with them. They have nuclear capability, and they're semi-intelligent. So we must tread softly until we can get the fuel we need to get off this hostile planet!" Now he's talking a little louder. He's got their attention. "I've tried unsuccessfully to contact Nibiru and the new planet. Neither is responding just yet, but I'm confident they will soon. I'm not through trying either. I've also considered requesting that perhaps the next transport could save us by bringing fuel." (He glances angrily at Kornak.) "But I feel it would be too risky to bring another ship here. We'll have to continue with our current emergency plan of finding gold on this planet to use for fuel. Mezruh and Orsello are currently out there searching the area. I hope they're okay. The gold will probably be elusive. I'm not sure what these beings use it for, except decoration. But we'll find out more. And if our comrades' mission is unsuccessful, we will continue to send parties out until we find what we seek. As long as we are camouflaged well and our manna machine stays functional, we will survive. Our search teams will find the gold we need to get us out of here. I'll take questions or suggestions at this time."

After a short silence (Kornak knows not to speak), Adria has a suggestion. Yes, she's been waiting to bring this up. She knows it has nothing to do with gold or survival, so she's not sure if she should. She thinks to herself, *Here goes!* She starts very hesitantly, "Commander

Zilog, sir, I know this is a dire situation and I don't mean to wander from this fact but . . ." She stops and looks away, unsure if she should continue.

Zilog encourages, "Continue, Adria. What is it?"

Adria responds, "Well, sir, as you know, our planet has been barren of domestic pets since the first war. No one could bring their beloved pets into any of the fallout shelters. I'm sure you remember it, sir." Zilog nods his head yes as Adria continues, her eyes welling up a little as she speaks. "Everyone lost their pets. I wasn't there of course. I wasn't born yet. But my grandmother told me about it. How sad it was. They put them in cages and left them there to die." Adria is talking with great passion now, almost crying as she speaks, "I've seen pictures, and I've heard others tell stories about them and how loving and playful they were." She turns directly to Zilog with her request. "Sir," she hesitates and then continues, "I know it may be out of line to even bring up pets, knowing we're in a life-threatening situation. But if we could take dogazoids to the new planet, well wouldn't it just be grand?" Her voice is getting excited, and she waves her hands with expression and excitement. (She loves this subject!) "We could surprise them on our arrival! Oh, think of the joy it would bring, sir! If we could find some . . . whew!" She pauses, smiling, looking a little dizzy. "We could sure bring some joy to the new planet."

Zilog listens intently for he too has a heart for pets. He was a young man when he had to leave his beloved dog behind. He remembers thinking it was a stupid rule that no pets were to be saved.

He speaks, "It's a good idea, Adria. I'm behind you on it, but we can't place it at top priority. Also, we don't yet know if there are any domestic pets here. But I like the idea. We shall pursue it, if we find it possible."

Adria bringing up the prospect of searching for dogs (or dogazoids as they were once known) gives Zilog a very unpleasant flashback, to the days of his youth. Here's what came to his mind . . .

As the countries on Nibiru devastated each other with nuclear bombs, all survivors and refugees were hurriedly rushed to fallout shelters, for survival. Zilog remembers the confusion and panic and saw many wounded people (mostly radiation wounds and dismemberment).

All had to wait in line to get into the deep underground refuge. In the distance, bombs could be heard.

Death loomed all around. Bodies lay about. Red dust swirled in the air as the atmosphere deteriorated.

Zilog doesn't like this unpleasant memory. But someone (Adria) opened that door in his mind and let it out. Now he's having it run through one more time.

It goes on with him, as a much younger, almost adolescent being standing in line for the fallout shelter.

He's wearing a heavy jacket with the collar turned up around his face. Others around him in line were also wearing heavy clothes and carrying their belongings. The mood was bleak.

Dust and debris swirled around making the air foul. (Did I already say that?) So he's standing in this line holding his suitcase in one hand. In the other hand, he's carrying Hiram, his beloved little dog. Hiram was small enough to carry, a Chihuahua mix. He was loyal and fun and loved to play. Zilog loved him so much.

Up ahead in the line, Zilog could see other people with dogs. They were stopping at a temporary building on the right and giving their dogs to someone there. There was a window and a counter that others were passing their dogs through to the officials in the building. Zilog thought, *This must be a safe place for pets during evacuation.* As he got closer, he could see that the ones who were turning over their pets were crying and arguing with the officials as they turned over their animals. Zilog could tell that this was not a good thing going on up there.

As he got closer, he realized that pets were being "taken away" and caged in a big wall of cages inside the temporary building. People were crying, some hysterically. Zilog asked the group ahead of him what might be going on with all the loud crying and such. The guy in front of him in line turned around and saw that Zilog was carrying a dog. With a sad expression, he looked up at Zilog and said, "You can't bring him in. They're exterminating all pets. None are to go to fallout."

Young Zilog was totally shocked! He couldn't believe his ears. How could they do this? He loved his little buddy! *This can't be happening*, he thought. He looked down at Hiram under his arm. He didn't want to lose him! He heard others crying around him, and it caused him to hold Hiram closer with both hands. He began to weep like those around him. *What should I do?* he thought to himself. *Should I get out of this line? Should I protest loudly at the window like the others I see doing it?* He chose not to. He did hold Hiram even closer. And he was crying openly when he got to the window counter. He grudgingly passed Hiram to the guy.

Hiram looked back at his daddy as he's being carried to a cage. He looked like he didn't know what's going on. Zilog kept crying as he moved on in the line, now just holding a suitcase, his other arm empty where Hiram used to be. Zilog could hear his beloved pal barking as he moved on in line. He couldn't stop crying.

As Zilog comes out of his nightmarish flashback, his eyes are watery. Go figure.

He hates that memory so much. He wishes people wouldn't open that door.

So the commander rallies his troops so to speak (gets their attention). They've been chatting while Zilog flashed back for a few moments. But he's back now, and he wants to talk some more.

He speaks, "Okay, guys, (he holds his hand up briefly) let's go ahead and break this up. I wanted you all to know the dangers of this environment and what we're doing to get through our situation." As they are filing out (still listening of course), he has more to say. "Oh and Adria, I like the idea about the dogs," he says cheerfully. He really must!

Adria gets a little tingle–chill when he says that! She's so excited about him liking her idea.

She doesn't know that he's speaking from a broken heart. But she still wants to keep talking about it. She has such a passion for dogs, even though she's never seen one.

Everyone has come to a standstill now, not quite out the door. Zilog and Adria are still yacking about dogs. Zilog continues, "This planet looks to me to be a place for such things. But let's look into the gold thing first though. Maybe after that we'll concentrate on less-pressing issues."

Adria doesn't know how to respond. She's sort of "caught in the headlights," so she just blurts out "Yes, sir." She wishes to say more but holds her tongue. She knows her commander can be short- tempered, and she doesn't want to push her subject (dogazoids) any further, not right now anyway. But she is ecstatic that Zilog thinks it's a good idea. She wants so bad to have a little doggie. She wants everyone to have one.

Zilog speaks one last time, "You guys are dismissed, for real this time. Go back to your jobs. Check on that manna machine. Make sure it's cleaned properly and loaded for tomorrow morning's meal."

Beltran and Melomar both turn toward Zilog and say "Yes, commander!" at the same time.

The crew disperses, and Zilog returns to looking at more "Earth facts" on his monitor. Maps tell him where gold has been found before, in ancient times. *What good is that?* he thinks.

He needs to know where gold is now—in this day and age. But his information-gathering device does not have any updated information. This is a hostile planet. No research has been done.

(Did I already say that?)

CHAPTER 2

AS MEZRUH AND ORSELLO WALK on a trail in the woods across from the feedstore, they discuss what went wrong with the carjacking (stealing).

Mezruh exclaims, "Whoo! I'm sorry. I just freaked. I didn't have enough time to study it."

Orsello replies, "I know, Mez. It's okay. You sure had my heart rate going good for a while. We'll get one though."

"Should we keep trying? It looks like it's going to be dark soon."

Mezruh points toward the sun which is near the horizon, or "almost down" as we call it. Orsello looks to where Mezruh is pointing and sees that his buddy is right. The sun's almost down.

Orsello replies, "We could stay out a while longer. We haven't done anything yet, ya know?"

"I'd like to at least show some progress for our commander. He's had a rough day."

"So let's stay out a while longer. See what we can find," says Orsello.

They stay in the woods (walking) parallel to town until they come to another road that intersects. At this point, our two heroes decide it's a good idea to morph into different human figures, other than the ones that were trying to steal a car down at the feedstore. So they agree to go old with it. They exchange shirts too—very tricky. They look convincing as two older gentlemen, just walking into town, minding their own business, chatting, laughing, and a little play fighting. It's all normal old guy behavior. If only the people of this little town knew whom these guys really are—aliens, from another planet, trying to steal stuff!

So they're walking toward town. It's almost dark now. (It's not that it really matters, just painting the picture for you readers. I love ya!) They're walking toward a traffic light.

They don't know what it is, only that it's bright and colorful. Cars are going by, and that excites them! Buildings also amaze our boys. On Nibiru almost everything is underground, for a long time now. You know why. There's almost nothing on the surface of the planet, except maybe doggy skeletons. Anyway, the guys really like the buildings, looking between them, looking at windows and door stoops. Things that we think nothing of, they think are amazing!

It's because they don't have it. They're so used to living inside the planet they don't know what it's like to exist on the outside, with buildings and cars. Don't forget the cars.

They hang a right at the light and keep walking. Cars (and trucks) are everywhere. Our heroes are shopping with their eyes. But they can't take anything now though. There are too many people around. These guys might not be very good at this, but they know the basics. You don't want to be stealing if there are people all around. Duh! It sure didn't work at the feedstore.

So the boys agree to sit down on a bench, in a pretty little park near the middle of town, just two old dudes setting on a bench, passing the evening away.

Who could tell that they're looking to steal a truck and then load it with more stolen stuff—(dare I say it) gold? So far it hasn't happened, but these guys just got here. They're bound to get better at it. They better anyway. They've got to get out of this place!

Zilog is worried. He is still looking at his maps and charts, but he's worried about his guys out there. There's no telling what kind of hell they're getting into. He sits back in his chair and rubs his eyes.

He doesn't want to think about what got them here. He's sick of being mad about it. He's also tired of wondering where the gold is on this mean little planet. *Maybe,* he thinks to himself, *he could contact his men in the field to see if there is anything to report and if they are okay* (of course).

So he holds his hand up to his face, the one with the communicative device implanted in it.

He speaks to it, "A calling B, A calling B. Come in, B. Over."

In the park in town Mezruh's hand device lights up without making any noise. He looks around to make sure no one is watching him talk to his hand. He speaks softly into his hand, which he has balled into a fist in front of his face.

Mezruh answers the call, "Hello, captain! I'm receiving your transmission well."

"I'm glad we have good frequency. Do you have any news from your exploration?"

"I'm sorry, sir, but so far we have not had much success. We're staked out in a small town, waiting for an opportunity to acquire a vehicle and then continue the mission, seeking gold non-forcefully." (He rolls his eyes when he says nonforcefully.)

"Very good! (He answers with false enthusiasm.) Continue with your exploration. Don't get hurt. I need you two. Don't interact with these beings if you can help it. And if you do, be careful. They are dangerous."

Mezruh acknowledges, "Orders received, sir. We'll be careful."

"Very good then. Over and out."

Mezruh didn't tell Zilog about their earlier attempt. Why bother? It didn't go well, so why mention it?

As Mezruh pulls his hand back down to his lap, he says to Orsello, "He (Zilog) thinks these people are dangerous and they're about to jump at us any time (a tone of sarcasm in his voice)."

Orsello responds, "I'm not seeing it. They look friendly to me, except for those guys earlier (at the feedstore). They looked mad."

"Yeah, we sort of had that coming. It'll get better though. Think positive."

So the night goes on a little while, as they sit on this bench watching cars go by. But then their concentration is interrupted by an older gentleman who walks up to them and just starts talking. Our boys weren't expecting this at all. They didn't want to talk to anybody. But this guy just starts rambling at them. He goes, "These bushes are coming in so nice." He waves his hand in front of a row of bushes. He goes on, "Some of 'em got that fungus disease. It kills 'em. But we been keeping up with it." Neither of the aliens answers. They don't know what to make of this guy. So he keeps right on talking, "Do you see that maple tree over there?" Now he's pointing and babbling about some tree. "We planted that tree seven springs ago in honor of . . ." Blah, blah, blah. Mezruh and Orsello look at each other as the guy goes on and on. It's clear they need to get away from him. He won't stop talking! So they both stand up from their seats and start to move on. But the talkative guy is disappointed that they are leaving, and he asks them to walk him back to the home.

Mezruh and Orsello look at each other (again). Orsello asks the guy, "Where is the home you come from?"

The old guy says, "It's two blocks that way (he points) and then hang a left, and it's down that street a bit."

The older guy seems to be sure of himself. He doesn't seem like he is a threat, so the aliens (shhhh, I mean "men") agree to walk with him. They aren't doing much anyway, just sitting around. At least now they are moving. As they walk, the older gentleman carries the conversation. He won't shut up! "This spot right here (he points down at the street) is where me and Bessie Martin used to park, across from the general store. I had a 1956 Ford that could really haul some groceries. I'm telling you what! That Bessie Martin, she could kiss like nothing I ever kissed before!" He is getting pretty excited with his story, talking loud. The boys are getting a kick out of it, glancing at each other and smiling as they walk. They are just three old guys walking down the street, one guy babbling and gesturing with his hands incessantly.

Back on board the ship . . .

The passengers have been assembled in the cafeteria area to hear the commander speak. Zilog steps into the room, and they give him applause. He looks magnificent in his commander's uniform and shiny boots. He raises his hand and smiles.

The crowd quiets as he begins to speak, "As you know, we have landed unexpectedly on a planet we know little about. Our ship is concealed in camouflage, so we are safe. We are also in a sparsely populated area. That is to say there aren't many of this planet's beings in this area. They're called humans, and they may be dangerous. My order is for you all to stay inside the ship."

One person in the audience asks rather loudly, "Why did we land here, commander?"

Zilog calmly responds, "We had a fuel problem, a leak." (He told them it was a leak even though he and the crew knew that it was Kornak's fault. It wasn't leakage at all.) He tells them next about how the leak was fixed and all they have to do now is to replace the lost fuel. He speaks, "The element that we need is here on this planet. We have only to find it and get it back here. We have the equipment we need for vaporization, so that won't be a problem. Currently I have a party of men, two men, seeking the raw material we need which is gold."

"Gold?!" someone in the audience says loudly.

Someone else also asks loudly, "Did somebody steal it, sir?" A little murmur falls over the crowd.

Zilog looks annoyed. He continues speaking, anyway, but louder, though, "Once we have enough melted and vaporized, we can leave this place and continue on our journey to H-2 (the new planet). I ask for your patience as we overcome this slight setback. My crew is a good crew, and we will get out of this!" The crowd seems to be reassured. Commander Zilog speaks well. His words soothe. He can speak with confidence because he believes it will happen.

So anyway, he resummons the attention of the passengers for one last instruction, "Friends, friends," he says raising his hand, "I need to say one more thing. In the event of our capture . . ." (the crowd doesn't like hearing that). He goes on, "I know. I know. I don't want to think about it either! But we are not prepared to fight. We are peaceful. Hopefully diplomacy can help us in a hostile situation. Let's just not get slaughtered by resisting. We don't want that! And we don't know what to expect, so we expect the worst. Again, I have to discuss this with you. But I don't by any means expect us to have to surrender to these beings. We are doing well so far, and as I said we will prevail and overcome (his voice getting louder), because I say we will!"

The passengers listen to Zilog's words intently, assured that things would end up well.

Even when he is faced with adversity, he remains strong. "Oh, yes," he says holding his hand up one last time. "It occurs to me that it will be better for all of us to shape-shift into this human form, just in case we are discovered. I feel that if they see us in our original form, it could frighten them enough to kill us all—nuke us or something. So let's go ahead and look like them just to be safe, in case we do have to mingle with this race."

(Break in the action you crazy sci-fi readers.)

This language that we call "English" has become universal. Many alien forms use it as their own. On our planet we call it English, but other races have other names for it. Nevertheless, many races use this dialect, with separate names for it. Sometimes different accents become a bit hard to understand (like an American listening to a British person talk), but overall the language is the same.

So anyway, let's get back to our story.

After ordering the passengers to morph to human form, Zilog himself does so, making himself a middle-aged maybe older-looking guy but distinguished.

He looks perhaps like Tom Hanks. How cool is that? You're gonna make yourself look good, right? Everyone else looks good too (as humans).

Zilog speaks (one last time), "We all look very good in this image! Heck, yeah! We can pull this off! But stay in the ship, until further notice. Thank you all for your attention. We'll speak again soon."

Everyone slowly begins to get up and head to the exits, talking among themselves about the meeting and their situation in general, a lotta mumbling and grumbling.

After speaking with the passengers, Zilog returns to the ship's helm and takes his seat.

He starts thinking about how the meeting went. He thinks, *I believe I spoke well and remained optimistic throughout. I will keep my passengers informed during this ordeal.*

As he is thinking these thoughts, the silence is broken by Kornak entering the room.

Kornak speaks (nervously), "Commander Zilog, sir, may I speak with you?" (Kornak knows to use military titles and protocol when approaching his uncle. Things will go much smoother.)

Zilog speaks, looking annoyed, "What is it, Kornak?"

Kornak, "Earlier today when we—the crew—met, Corporal Slosser (Adria) spoke of seeking domestic pets, and I saw that you were interested."

Zilog (still sounding impatient) replies, "Yes, we all miss our pets, but we don't know yet if this planet has such animals. It would be something worth looking into." He looks away as he talks. He's still mad.

Then Zilog's voice changes from gruff to softer as he asks Kornak his next question.

With a sad look on his face, Zilog asks him, "How could you overlook fueling the ship? We all put our trust in you. Now here we sit on some hostile planet (his voice rising in anger)! How could you?!"

Kornak has no answer. He looks down at the floor and wishes he had never come in here.

He begins to speak softly, "Sir, I'd like to volunteer to search for animals of domestic value." He goes on, "I know, sir, that it won't make up for what I've caused. But I want to try."

Zilog stares angrily. Kornak returns to staring at the floor. There is so much tension in the air.

Finally, Zilog speaks up, still talking loud because he's still mad, "How do I know you're not going to screw up looking for pets too? I understand that you want to redeem yourself and make up for your mistakes. But I'm angry with you. You let us all down, and now we may have to pay with our lives. I covered for you in there (he gestures toward the passenger area). I told them that the fuel leaked out through an undetected pinhole! I told them that, just so you wouldn't look like a fool fit to be prosecuted! I hope your blunder won't cost us all our lives! Leave me now, Kornak. You're dismissed!" Kornak turns without speaking and exits the bridge area. He wonders if the commander had intentionally not answered his request. Or perhaps it was just "no" when he talked about screwing it up. Either way, it was "no," and Kornak knew to leave it alone. He returns to his quarters trying to think of a way to make it up to his uncle and his comrades.

Meanwhile, Zilog is still angry. That little exchange with Kornak riled him up. He broods for a little while and then comes up with what he wants to do. He thinks to himself, *Why not send the kid out? Let him see what he can find.* He hates to think of his nephew as expendable, but in his current state of anger, it seems like a good idea. Two of his crewmembers are already out "exploring," and he surely doesn't want to lose them. But this Kornak kid has been like a bad luck story all his life. Zilog thinks, *Maybe I could send him out just to get rid of him for a while. Perhaps he could even redeem himself by doing something good. Or maybe he'll get captured by these beings and never be seen or heard from again. Hmmm,* he thinks, *that sounds good.*

But he thinks awhile longer, and eventually his mood gets a little better. He still loves the kid.

And he doesn't consider Kornak "expendable." That was just mad talk—no more of that.

So Zilog goes ahead and summons Kornak back to the bridge. He wants to talk.

As Kornak arrives moments later, he looks afraid, ready to be chewed out again.

But Zilog's mood has improved. He seems calm, calm enough to give orders. He speaks, "After consideration, I've decided that you will be suitable to go in search of domestic pets. But your mission will also include searching for gold to power the ship. And you must travel alone, Kornak. I can't spare anyone else to go out. And I believe you will do best by shape-shifting to the form of a child . . . no . . .

an adolescent human. Animals trust people of that age more readily. I remember it."

Kornak nods yes while saying "Yes, sir."

Zilog keeps going, "You should leave when that sun of theirs shows up on the eastern horizon. Move with the light of day (what we call morning)."

One more hearty "Yes, sir!" from Kornak as he snaps to attention enthusiastically, and Zilog dismisses him. They both share a smile, and Zilog wishes him luck.

Meanwhile, back in town, Mezruh and Orsello are walking their new friend back to his place of residence—the local retirement home. He hasn't stopped talking all the while. But his words are harmless, mostly reminiscing the past. The aliens are patient, pretending to be interested, but looking around at all the vehicles everywhere. They need one of them bad boys. There aren't nearly as many humans as there were in the middle of town. The possibilities are growing.

As the three men approach the "Sunshine Retirement Home," the boys' new friend invites them for coffee on the porch. There is a group of elderly people gathered on the porch having coffee and socializing. Mezruh and Orsello are apprehensive, but they agree to stop in. The people are very pleasant. They serve the boys coffee (which they are unfamiliar with), and the introductions begin. The man whom they had met in town and walked home with sticks his hand out to shake with Orsello and says his name is Earl. Orsello hesitates a few moments and introduces himself as Rob. As they shake hands, "Rob" gestures toward Mezruh and says, "This is my friend, Bob."

Earl repeats their names as they shake hands, "Bob and Rob is it?"

"That's us," Mezruh answers. "Bob and Rob."

Next, a lady steps into the group holding her hand up to be kissed. She introduces herself as Emily. She has her hand up in front of Orsello, so he takes it and says, "Nice to meet you, ma'am."

Mezruh nods in agreement. They both notice the ornaments on her hand and wrist. Their eyes light up! Gold!

But the introductions go on. Bob and Rob have some new friends—Dan, Tom, Lydia, and Warren, all very nice people. One of the ladies asks where Bob and Rob are from and what brings them to their town. Bob and Rob don't have an immediate response to the questions, but Mezruh comes up with one shortly. He goes, "We . . . um . . . are here to visit my relatives."

"Well that's nice," Lydia says. "Who are they?"

Orsello changes the subject by complementing the house. "This is a lovely home you have here. You must work hard to keep it so." It was all he could think of to say, but it worked. All their new friends start talking at the same time—all about their wonderful home.

Mezruh thinks to himself, *My, how these humans like to socialize!*

So they all converse for a while, and when their coffee cups are empty, Bob and Rob are a little anxious to say their goodbyes. They need to move on with their mission. They need a vehicle, and they need gold. Standing here on this porch isn't getting anything done. They are nice people though. So they all say goodbye, and our boys go on their way.

Mezruh mumbles as they head back toward town, "Did you see the gold on that lady's hand?"

"Heck, yeah I did," Orsello responds sounding excited. "But how are we supposed to obtain it without violence?"

"I know. I know," Mezruh responds. "I felt like morphing into something big and mean and ripping her arm off!"

"That's no good though," Orsello reminds him. "Zilog gave us his orders: no force, no violence."

Mezruh asks, "Yeah, but how are we supposed to do that?"

Orsello responds, "I don't know yet, but we can't just grab and run. It takes time to liquefy the gold and then vaporize it. We can't do it with a bunch of these guys chasing us."

Mezruh answers, "I bet we could. These beings don't look very dangerous. But orders are orders. Zilog is already mad at that new kid for causing all this. We darn sure don't want his wrath on us! We've got to find a way."

Just then an armored truck goes by. They both notice it—big heavy-duty-looking thing.

On the side is written "Goldstein Armored Services." But all Mezruh sees is the word "gold"!

This falsely tells them that this big truck is full of gold! That's what they think anyway.

"Holy moley!" Mezruh says kind of loud. "There's our gold right there!" He's excited! "We've got to follow it! Don't let it out of your sight, partner!"

The truck rolls through the downtown area and pulls in at the bank, which is closed. The armored service is here to pick up the day's deposits, on its normal route. But on this evening, there are two shady-looking old men watching from the sidewalk. The driver pulls up in front of the bank and gets out, as does the passenger. They are both wearing blue uniforms. They both have guns too. So they move to the back of the truck, and one opens the door, first unlocking it with his key. He reaches into the truck and pulls out a small hand truck. From where they are standing, Mezruh and Orsello can see two bags inside the truck, large canvas bags. But then the guard closes the door. And with that, the two guards walk toward the bank's front doors.

Our heroes look at each other, amazed by their apparent good fortune. As the guards proceed into the bank, M and O are making their move. Knowing that the door would be locked, Mezruh puts his shape-shifting fingers into the door lock, and boom the driver door is open.

The engine is running, the way the driver left it. So Mezruh jumps in and quickly reaches to unlock the passenger door to let Orsello in. He jumps in acting very serious, no joyful laughter this time.

By now Mezruh is teaching himself what makes this thing move! He puts a hand on the shifter, and he sees the pedals on the floor. He doesn't want to mess this up again. So he puts his foot on the brake pedal, and the shifter glides down to "D" with the weight of his hand on it.

And they're off, moving! Mezruh holds the steering wheel like a pro and expertly steers the truck around the car parked in front of them. He can't believe it. They have a vehicle! And hopefully those big bags they saw in the back are full of gold.

Mezruh says, "We got one! I just knew we could do it!"

Orsello, equally happy, chimes in, "Heck, yeah! Let's get this thing back to the ship! I'll notify Commander Zilog. I'll tell him we're coming home! Woo! This is great!" He then raises his hand to his face and begins contacting Zilog. "Blue to red, blue calling red over."

On the ship, Zilog is startled by Orsello's call. He answers, "This is red. I'm receiving your transmission. Do you have good news for me, gentlemen?"

Orsello responds with much excitement in his voice, "Commander, we have a vehicle! Mezruh is operating it, and we think it may have gold in the back!" Zilog's eyes become wide when he hears about gold. He's excited now. He's happy that his guys are okay and really happy to hear about gold.

Zilog tells Orsello to pass on that the vehicle shouldn't be driven fast, so as not to draw attention to themselves. He tells them, "Just be careful and get that thing back here. Very good, gentlemen. I knew you could do it. The cargo bay ramp will be lowered for you. Approach the ship from that side and pull the vehicle into the ship."

"Orders received, sir," Orsello says, excitedly, concluding the conversation.

Back at the bank . . .

The guards come out with the day's deposits only to find their truck gone.

Both stand there in total surprise, looking at the spot where they had left it. One guy says, "Who could have done this?! This town doesn't have any crime."

"I know," says the other guy. He then pulls out his cell phone and calls their boss, "Hey, Frank, you're not going to believe this, but the truck got stolen. We're at the bank in Clemsdale. Yes, I locked it! I always lock it. I don't know how they got in it, but they sure did it fast! We were only inside the bank for about two minutes. I swear two minutes! We came out, and it was gone." He goes on, "Yes, there's money in it, the deposits from Wellsboro and Mansfield. I'd say about forty thousand dollars!"

Back in the stolen truck, our heroes are getting a bit giddy, although Mezruh tries to keep things serious, even though he is very happy and relieved that they landed something. He tells Orsello, "I'll take us back to our truck and drop you off. You get in it and follow me back to the ship. We've got to get our machine back home safely." Orsello agrees and soon they are back at the utility vehicle, and Orsello gets out. Luckily there is no one around snooping about. Orsello jumps in, and off they go.

After a few more minutes of driving, they are back at the field where the ship is hidden.

Mezruh, knowing that the trees are electronically produced, drives the truck right through them. To a normal human observer, it would look like the truck crashed into the trees and then disappeared, followed by a futuristic-looking army truck.

Mezruh pulls the armored truck right up into the ship. Orsello leaves the utility vehicle outside but jumps out fast to join the others in the cargo bay. He scurries up the ramp quickly.

Now the excitement level is high. Zilog and the rest of the crew have gathered in the cargo bay, a welcoming committee, along with several of the passengers.

Mezruh jumps out of the truck eagerly. He is very proud of his and Orsello's achievement.

He is talking fast as he walks to the back of the truck to unlock it, "We just saw an opportunity and jumped on it! I hope this thing has gold in it. We couldn't tell from a distance." He turns and talks directly to Zilog, "I hope there's gold in here, sir. It says gold right on the side."

By now he has shape-shifted his finger into the door lock and fiddles with it for a moment until it pops open. No one seems surprised that he did it so fast. He's learning quickly. As the door opens, they can see the two canvas bags. The rest of the truck is empty, just the two bags. Zilog, Mezruh, and Orsello jump up into the truck and hurry to the bags. Zilog opens one bag only to find paper currency. Mezruh opens the other bag to the same disappointment, paper. Everyone is dismayed as word comes out of the truck. There's no gold, just paper currency. It's very valuable to the people of this planet, but worthless to the ones who need gold to power their ship.

Zilog struggles to maintain his composure. Mezruh and Orsello are visibly angry. All was for nothing, just when they thought they had done so well.

All three exit the truck. Zilog speaks to the disappointed group, "These soldiers tried hard for us. We are let down, this time. But we will continue until we succeed! We just missed it this time. It hurt. We were all very hopeful. But we are strong, and this setback will soon be forgotten, and we will move forward." He stands tall and rigid as he speaks and sternly raises his fist in defiance and says, "We will overcome this!"

So Zilog dismisses everyone to their duties. As the group disperses, Zilog motions for Mezruh to stay back. Zilog needs him to move the armored truck outside, and then he will pull the utility truck back in, which he does. It takes a few minutes. And as he is getting out of the truck, Mezruh approaches him with an idea, "Commander, I have a suggestion."

Zilog perks up a little bit and says, "Let's hear it, Mezruh! We need some suggestions."

So Mezruh tells him, "I was thinking that the paper currency we have holds value. Perhaps we could trade it for gold. I know, sir, that we don't know the ways of the people here; but if we studied them and their habits, we could learn how to spend their money and where to trade it for gold. What do you think?"

Zilog says, "It's a good idea, but I don't want to mingle with them too much. They might turn on us if we are discovered to be not from here. Then they would probably kill us all. But I like your idea, and it's the only way we have to go. So go ahead and take some of that currency and let's see if we can learn how to use it."

They're unfamiliar with currency because their race hasn't used it for centuries. All monetary transactions are done electronically, like we have here on our planet, only they have evolved to the point of not needing currency any more, hundreds of years ago.

So anyway, Zilog goes over to the panel to close the door. He takes one last look outside. He looks at the money truck sitting there. "Dammit!" he says out loud. He pushes the button that closes the door. Up it goes. The cargo area is all dark now, kind of gloomy. Zilog and Mezruh head out, up the corridor that leads to the main control room, or bridge, where they end up. The commander summons the crew that he just dismissed, and he and Mezruh wait for them to report.

As they come shuffling in one at a time, the mood is pleasant and somewhat light. Kornak is still drawing dirty looks from everyone though.

Zilog, seeing that everyone is present, raises his hand and begins to speak, "An idea has been brought to my attention, and I'm sharing it with you. The paper currency we have acquired is not worthless. We can use it, hopefully to obtain the gold we need. But first we need to learn how to use it. It will take us some time to do this. Whoever goes on this mission (he looks around the room) will be in great danger and will have to stay very low key. We need to fit in and not look suspicious. And we definitely need to find where they buy and sell gold, as well as how much it costs." The crew listens intently. Zilog starts with the inspirational stuff, "We will get out of here. We just have to be patient. Our intelligence will prevail. Now, who wants to learn about paper currency on this planet?" Of course, all raise their hands. They are all brave and adventurous. (Did I already say that?)

After much consideration (about half a minute), Zilog decides on Mezruh and Orsello again since they did good on their first mission. The others don't look disappointed. Perhaps the safety of staying at the ship offers more security than mixing it up with the dangerous beings here. But Mezruh and Orsello are up for the job. After all they already made some friends here, and they seemed like nice people.

But they need a smaller vehicle. The big stolen armored truck is no good. They can't be driving that around. They need something that blends in. But first things first. Zilog instructs them to bring the bags of currency into the ship for safekeeping. It's theirs. They stole it fair and square. He also tells them to get up in the morning and take the armored truck back near where they got it from and ditch it. "Then go get something better. And then, once you're in that, go into the town you say is nearby. Take some of the currency and see how these people use it for trading. Watch and learn, guys. See what's involved. And always be on the lookout for gold, not to steal though! That's what the currency is for. So watch and learn, but don't draw attention to yourselves." After a few moments of silence, Zilog begins to end the meeting, "Are there any suggestions? Questions?" He looks around the room.

Adria perks up a little and says very quietly, "Requesting permission to seek domestic pets, sir."

Zilog responds, "I can't risk losing you, corporal. I know your intentions are sincere. But I need you in your capacity to fly this ship and maintain our food source. I haven't forgotten about looking into this. I planned to send Corporal Kornak to scout for such animals."

"Yes, sir," Adria answers sadly. She is disappointed, but Zilog made his decision, and she would in no way object. But she wonders if that Kornak kid can come back with anything. *Probably not*, she thinks.

"You are all dismissed," Zilog says rather loudly. Everyone turns toward the door and heads for it, like kids getting let out of school. "Have a good night, everyone!" the chief says.

7:00 a.m.! Earth time. Kornak is up and moving per his commander's orders. He's going on a conquest—in his mind, an epic conquest. He will be seeking gold to power the ship but also seek animals of domestic value. He is excited. And he's so happy to be back in Zilog's good graces. He thinks to himself, *I can't blow this assignment. I got to come back with something positive.*

Kornak is now ready to leave the ship. All is quiet as he slips out a side door normally used as an emergency exit. He's familiar with this door. He and another guy installed it, a couple of months ago, back on the home planet. Anyway, out the door he goes. The crisp morning air feels great in his lungs, as he strides through dew-soaked grass. *How unspoiled this planet is,* he thinks to himself. Then he thinks back to Nibiru and how everything is gone. Just red dirt is left. But this planet is beautiful! *Perhaps,* he thinks, *the beings here haven't made weapons powerful enough to destroy their planet's atmosphere . . . yet.*

As Kornak passes into the electronic forest, he stops for a second and morphs into an adolescent male human as his commander instructed. He starts out into the field eager to do something good. As he walks, he can hear a rumbling noise behind him. He turns to see what it is. And it's two old guys driving an armored truck. Kornak lets out a sigh of relief. He knows these guys. It's Mezruh and Orsello. They smile and wave to the kid walking. The kid waves back. When they reach the road, the truck goes south, and the kid goes north.

CHAPTER 3

MEZRUH AND ORSELLO (ALSO KNOWN as Rob and Bob) take the armored truck back to where they had ditched their utility vehicle the day before, a nice woodsy spot outside of town. They get out. Both have their old guy look going on. They both have money too, fifties and hundreds, lots of them.

So there they go again, walking up the road toward town, past the feedstore where they were unsuccessful yesterday. But today is a better day for them. They learned a little from their mishaps. They have some currency. They even have aliases. So Bob and Rob are definitely doing better today.

Going in the other direction on the same road is Kornak, also walking. He is very proud to be on a mission for his commander. If only he could be successful. *Got to find some gold and dogs too,* he thinks. He pumps himself up with positive reinforcement as he walks. "I can do this!" he says out loud. He's pretty excited about this assignment. He sure doesn't want to mess it up.

After a while of walking, Kornak comes to a neighborhood. He is unfamiliar with these aboveground dwellings. All dwellings on Nibiru are underground. Houses like this are a thing of the distant past.

So he approaches, following the street that leads to this strange new community. A car goes by. The driver and Kornak exchange glances. *No big deal,* he thinks. *People here seem peaceful.* As he walks further into the rows of houses, he sees more signs of life—a guy washing his car. He's got a radio playing music. Further down the street, Kornak sees a kid mowing a lawn. He smells the freshly mowed grass. He also hears the sound of the lawn mower.

Kornak is amazed by things that seem ordinary to us humans. *How beautiful this planet is*, he thinks. He hopes again their new home is this unspoiled.

Then he comes upon an open field between the rows of houses. And in this field are some kids playing loudly. Kornak stands and watches them as they play. It looks like a rough game, with some kind of a ball. *Hmmm*, he thinks, *I wonder what this is.*

One of the kids on the field sees Kornak standing there gawking at them. So the kid yells to him, "Hey, kid, get in here! We need one more!"

Kornak looks around to make sure the kid was talking to him. He then responds with, "Me? Sure, I'll play!"

As he jogs out to where the kids are gathered, he is very unsure about what he's doing.

When he arrives at the huddle, he sees them standing in a circle bent over. So he crowds into the huddle, bent over like the others. One kid is talking, giving orders, "Can you block that kid or not?" he says. "You two go across the middle. You (he points to Kornak), what's your name, kid?"

"Mike," Kornak blurts out.

"Okay then, Mike, I want you to go deep. Line up wide and go deep." He then yells loudly, "Ready. Break!" All join in yelling "break," startling Kornak. He wasn't expecting that. Everyone hustles to the line of scrimmage, where the other team is waiting. Kornak (Mike) is kind of confused. He's still standing where the huddle was, looking lost. He is unsure where he is supposed to be. The kid who called the play looks at him and repeats, "Line up wide and go deep, Mike! C'mon. Let's go. Chop chop!"

Line up wide and go deep, Kornak thinks. *What does that mean?* The kid at the end of the offensive line looks at Kornak (Mike) and points to where he is supposed to be. So Kornak jumps to it and jogs out to where the kid was pointing, and the play starts. The kid who called the play now has the ball, and he's motioning Kornak to run.

So Kornak takes off, a bit late but he runs down the field. The kid launches a big pass. Kornak assumes he's supposed to catch it. So without much effort, he runs under it and makes the catch. Touchdown! Everyone on his team is cheering and jumping around. "Whoo-hoo! Nice going, new kid!" They're laying it on a little thick for him, since he's new. If only they knew who he really is and why he's here.

Although he just scored a touchdown, he still doesn't know anything about this game. But he wants to learn. After the touchdown celebration is over, the game goes on. Mike seems very out of place to the other kids. He doesn't know anything at all about this game. *How can that be?* they wonder. But he is eager to learn. He asks questions that seem obvious, but the kids are more than happy to answer. He seems like a novelty to them. *A big kid who doesn't know anything about football? That's just crazy,* they all think. *Where is he from another planet or something?* (Maaaybe.)

After one play, the ball goes over a fence into someone's yard. All the kids are disappointed. They all know whose yard it is. And a big mean dog lives there. Luckily one of the kids playing football lives there too, so he has to go in the fence to get the ball. His name is Lionel. Everyone yells his name to go get the ball. Mike watches intently. He's not sure what's going on here. Obviously, there's a reason no one goes in that fence, except Lionel.

So Kornak watches as Lionel goes up to the gate. At the sound of the gate latch jangling, a loud bark is heard. Kornak isn't sure what this noise is, but he sees in just a second. From around the side of the house comes a giant dog barking like crazy. Kornak is astounded by this thing.

It's a bullmastiff, barking and slobbering as it runs up to Lionel. Kornak watches in amazement as the dog stops barking when he sees it is his owner. Lionel pets the big boy on his head. Kornak watches intently. *This must be a dog,* he thinks. It's big and mean looking. *Is this what Adria was talking about?* He had seen pictures of smaller ones, but this thing looks more like a monster! How is he supposed to get something like this back to the ship?

So anyway, Lionel pets the dog for a few seconds and then goes and gets the ball. Kornak is still watching the giant dog, as it goes back around the side of the house. *Unbelievable,* he thinks.

In the meantime, all the kids head back to the field to play some more ball. Kornak is glad he survived that episode without letting on that he'd never seen one of those (dogs) before. *Whew,* he thinks. *Close call.* They were already kind of suspicious when they found out that he didn't know anything about football. If the kids thought he'd never seen a dog before, he might blow his cover. So it's good that he didn't freak out when he saw it.

As he ponders these thoughts, the other kids are tossing the ball and talking crap with each other like they always do. Kornak likes this group of kids. They are funny and easy to get along with. He's glad he found them. So Kornak stays a little while longer, playing ball with these crazy kids, but then he has to continue with his mission. He doesn't tell them that of course. He just tells them he has a bunch of stuff to do, so he has to leave. He tells them, "I hate to leave such good company, but I really have to go."

As his new friends gather to say goodbye to Mike, they start shooting silly football questions at him. They're messing with him. They know he's not into football trivia. "Hey, Mike!" one yells. "Who's your favorite team? Don't have one, do ya? Who you got winning the Super Bowl, Mike?"

Mike is laughing and looking down as the questions fly by.

"Who's gonna win the big dance?"

One kid holds up his hand like he's showing off a ring. He says, "Who's gonna win the gold? Those big gold rings."

Kornak perks up when he hears the word gold. "What's that about gold?" he inquires.

One kid named Wes speaks up, "The team that wins the Super Bowl gets big gold rings. You didn't know that, Mike? Big ole rings, I ain't lying."

Kornak asks, "For playing this game here? Football?"

All nod their heads yes.

"Gold you say?" he asks again.

"Yup," one kid says. "Solid gold."

"That's really something," Kornak responds, his eyes looking sort of watery. "Gold?" He looks hypnotized for a few seconds as the kids stare at him. He mumbles, "We could win gold playing this football game."

"Yeah and there's a cool trophy too," one kid says. "But it's not gold though, just those rings."

Mike says, "I bet those guys are some good football players."

"Yeah, they are," one of the kids says. "Last year it was the Patriots."

Mike looks surprised. "It happens every year? They give gold to the winner every year?"

"Yup, every year, bro," the kid answers.

"Wow! That's amazing," he (Kornak) says. "So every year one team wins the Super Bowl, and the whole team gets gold rings?"

All the kids nod their heads yes. It's starting to get redundant.

One kid asks, "How can you not know all this, Mike? Whatta ya live under a rock or something?"

Another kid throws in, "No, he's from another planet!" Everyone laughs.

Kornak laughs too and says, "I do stay home a lot. It's nice to get out. Thanks for teaching me, you guys."

With that they all say goodbye, and Kornak turns to walk away. But he stops and turns back to them and asks, "Do any of you guys know where I can get a little dog? My mom lost her little dog. Is there any place around here where I can get one? Nothing like that thing though!" He points to the big dog's yard. Most of the kids shrug their shoulders and say they don't know of any.

But one kid does! He knows where the dog pound is! He tells Kornak, "They've got all kinds of dogs there. Take your mom and let her pick one out herself."

"Where is it?" Kornak asks with excitement.

The kid starts rambling, "Well, let me see. I'm not from around here. I'm from the other side of town. I'd be coming from the other way. I'm here visiting my cousin Cody." Cody raises his hand.

Kornak is looking a little impatient. "Do you guys know where this place is?" he asks.

"It's coming to me now," the first kid says. "You go out here to the main highway (he's pointing toward the road Kornak was on) and you get on that road. You go about a half a mile, and there will be a light." Kornak listens intently. He's not sure what a light is, but he's still listening. So the kid goes on, "You hang a right at that light, and it's only about half a block down on the right-hand side." Kornak doesn't know what a block is, but he thinks he can figure it out. He's excited, telling the kid to go over it again. "Main road, half a mile, right at the light, down a little ways on the right."

Another kid says, "You got this, Mike! Take your mom there. She'll love it."

Kornak answers all excited, "I will! Thank you, guys!"

He turns and starts walking, his head full of ideas. Should he go back to the ship now?

He decides against it since he has nothing to show so far and the day is not over.

But he does have some information he wants to share with his commander. You know that stuff about football players getting gold for winning the . . . what was it . . . the Super Dish? Hmmm, that's not it . . . Super Bowl? There it is—Super Bowl. And also, he can't wait to see this dog place.

So Kornak gets back to the main road and goes like the kid told him to. He sees something hanging over the road up ahead. It's flashing different colors. Kornak thinks, *That must be the "light" that the kid was talking about.* He also sees a lot of cars going by, but they don't bother him. He knows he looks normal to these beings, so he fits in just fine. He's not drawing attention or anything, just a kid walking down the road on the sidewalk.

As Kornak gets closer to the light, he hears dogs barking. But he's not sure what it is he's hearing. The only dog he's heard bark was that big ole dog with his woof woof style. This sounds different— higher-pitched yaps.

And then he sees it, off to his right! There's a long fence-looking structure and inside it are . . . bingo . . . dogs! Kornak freezes. He's staring at the dogs with disbelief. There are lots of them, different sizes and kinds. Most of them are barking and looking happy.

So Kornak keeps walking until he reaches "the light" the kid talked about. He turns right, and he can see the place now. It's a red brick building with glass in front. Kornak eagerly goes through the glass door to the inside, where he sees a counter with a girl standing behind it.

He tells her the story about his mom losing her dog. She feels sorry, and she assures him that he has come to the right place. She leads him out to where the rows of cages are. Again Kornak is amazed. Now that he can see them up close, he is amazed by the beauty of these animals. He thinks to himself, *How could our ancestors have done away with such beautiful creatures? No wonder Adria feels the way she does about these things.*

So Kornak pulls himself together and starts asking the girl questions. He asks, "What do I do to get one of these?"

The girl answers pleasantly, "Well, the price is thirty-five dollars each. They all get neutered or spayed."

Kornak asks, "All sizes are the same price?"

"Yes," the girl says, "thirty-five dollars." Kornak tells her that he'll have to come back. She tells him, "You can bring your mom and let her pick one out if you want to." Kornak thanks her for being so helpful, and he leaves, once again walking. But now he's ready to go back to the ship. He's made some progress, by finding dogs, and he has stories about gold for playing the Earth game they call football!

Meanwhile, Orsello and Mezruh are doing fine (in case you were worried). They've walked back to town, and now they are trying to decide which store they are going to go in to spend some money! They've decided to sit down on a bench (again) for a few minutes and talk this over.

Mezruh says, "I hope that Earl guy doesn't come up and start babbling again."

Orsello is looking at storefronts but listening. He says to his buddy, "He was an okay guy. He just talks too much! I think that's a food store down on the end there." He nods his head toward it.

Mezruh says, "I sort of noticed it, but there are a lot of humans going in and out of it, too crowded." Then Mezruh perks up a little and starts reading storefront signs on the row of stores across the street. "Let's see . . . grocery store, drug store, toy store, jewelry store, phone store."

"Wait. Wait. Wait," Orsello says a little too loud. "What was that last one? Jewelry?"

Mezruh cranks his head back a notch and says, "Yep, jewelry. I'm not sure what that means."

Orsello sounds a little angry, "You don't know what it means?" Mezruh points at the jewelry store and sounds out the word, "Jew-el-ry. What's it mean already?"

Orsello sounds excited as he speaks, "That's where the gold is! Jewelry is made out of gold! You didn't know that? That's it! That's where we need to go!"

So they get up from their roost (bench) and head across the street to the jewelry store, pockets full of money. Here goes another crazy encounter!

The door jingles as they walk into the jewelry store. Bob and Rob are both nervous as hell.

"Good morning, gentlemen," says the nice lady behind the glass counter. "What can I help you with today?" Her glass counter has golden trinkets inside. Both of our boys are glancing at it!

Mezruh starts bumbling out their request, "Um we'd . . . we'd um . . . like to see some gold."

Orsello nods in agreement and joins in, "Yeah, we'd like to see some gold."

The lady responds looking surprised, "Well then, what type of gold would you like today? A bracelet? Ring maybe? We also have watches and necklaces. We have many variations of gold, for all needs and occasions. Is there an occasion of some kind?"

Orsello takes this one, "An occasion? Yes, there's an occasion. The occasion is . . ."

"Birthday," Mezruh chimes in. He saw a poster on the wall that said something about birthday. He doesn't know what birthday means. But he goes with it. He thinks to himself, *Now we're getting somewhere.* "Someone very dear to us," Mezruh blurts out, not giving any details.

"Well," she says, "is it a man or a woman? What kind of gold do you think they would like?"

She's getting a little annoyed, but she doesn't want to miss making a sale. So she remains patient with these old weirdos. They seem very odd.

Mezruh gets brave and changes the subject slightly, "Do you have just gold by itself? Gold that hasn't been made into anything?"

She looks puzzled. She's never had a request like this. She says, "Gold just by itself?" repeating his words. "Hmm, gold just by itself," she says over again. She thinks to herself, *This confirms it. These dudes are nuts.* So she tells them, "I don't think we have it in that form, but let me check with my associate."

The helpful lady goes behind a curtain in a doorway and leaves our boys mumbling to each other. Orsello is leaning all over the glass counter looking suspicious. He says, "I don't think they have what we want. It's all this little stuff (he points down at some watches). We need more quantity!"

Mezruh answers, "This gold has all been made into trinkets and adornment. You're right. This isn't what we want. We definitely need more quantity. Should we just get out of here?"

Orsello objects saying, "Let's just wait. See what she has to say."

So the lady comes back through the curtain, with an older gentleman (looks kind of like Doc on *Gunsmoke*) following her. He approaches our boys with a look of disbelief. He says, "You boys want raw gold?"

Mezruh says, "Yes, that's what we need." He starts lying, "We need it to make our own ornamental statue."

After a few awkward seconds of silence, the man says, "Well, I'm sorry, gentlemen. We don't have gold in raw form."

Orsello looks disappointed but stays cordial saying, "Oh, well. We thought we'd ask. I guess we'd like to buy some of this stuff," pointing down at the gold rings.

The man and woman look at each other puzzled. He tells her, "Sell these gentlemen some gold, Marjorie! Pull these trays out and let these good men pick what they like!"

So Marjorie pulls out a velvet tray with a row of rings and begins her sales pitch, "These are wedding bands of varying sizes. These over here have diamonds."

"No, thanks on the diamonds," Mezruh tells her, "just gold."

"Okay," she says, "no diamonds, hmm. This row of rings are the heaviest ones we sell, probably what you're after." She's trying to comply to their needs, but inside she's becoming more suspicious of these two nutbags.

Mezruh, pointing at the rings, says, "How much for this row here?" "All of them?" she says surprised.

Orsello replies back, "Yeah, all of them. Can you give us a total?" She pulls out a little adding machine and starts punching the keys like crazy. As she's doing this, she notices both men are reaching into their pockets.

Oh no, she thinks, *is this going to be a robbery?* No, they both pull out wads of cash.

"Okay," she says. "Whew! For those five rings you chose, the total comes to 7,560 dollars." Both men look unsurprised because they don't know that's a lot of money. (If you remember, they were supposed to go slow and learn how to spend the money. They didn't.) They have bills, but both are unsure about counting them.

So these two crazy-acting old men are counting out big stacks of money. Marjorie can't believe this is happening. They're not counting very good, so she jumps in and sort of takes over. She knows this stuff. The boys have to pull more currency (as they call it) out of their pockets. But they've got it covered. Marjorie has a lot going through her head, *Who are these two? Pockets full of money? Looking for raw gold?* She doesn't know what to make of these guys. But she wants to make this sale, so she stays friendly and cordial. "Okay, boys," she says, "let me package these up for you. Get all this money put away, and you guys will be all set."

After a few awkward moments, she gives them a bag with five little white boxes in it. Everyone smiles and says goodbye to each other, and the two turn to leave. Even "Doc" comes out from the curtain to say goodbye.

"Have a nice day!" Marjorie sings out.

"You too," Mezruh mumbles. But then the door jingles! Someone is coming in. Wow! It's Lydia from the retirement home last night!

"Bob and Rob!" she says rather loudly. "How are you boys doing this morning?"

Marjorie picks up on Lydia knowing these guys. Marjorie and Lydia are good friends, but Marjorie wonders where Lydia knows these two whackos from. Bob and Rob answer Lydia very cordially. Bob says, "Hi, Lydia! How nice to see you."

Rob (Orsello) also seems pleased to see her. "Good morning, miss," he says a little too enthusiastically.

Lydia comes back with, "You boys in here shopping around a little?"

Bob (Mezruh) says, "Yes, miss, we sure are enjoying your lovely town." They step toward the door, anxious for this exchange to be over. Bob tells Lydia to have a good day.

"Okay," she says pleasantly.

They step out the jingling door. Mezruh has the bag with the gold in it. "Let's get out of here," he says.

"I'm with ya!" Orsello responds. So they walk down the street, past the row of shops toward the suburbs. Mezruh nonchalantly raises his hand and starts talking softly, "Red to blue, red to blue over."

Back on the ship, Zilog is visiting with some passengers in the cafeteria. He has also allowed them to go outside in small groups, to enjoy the lovely atmosphere of this planet. They've been instructed not to go outside the camouflage ring and to stay in human form for safety.

But right now, he has a communication coming in; and he turns away, holding up his hand to speak. He says, "This is blue. Come in, red. Over."

Mezruh is excited. "Commander! We have some good news!"

Zilog gets a happy look on his face and proclaims, "Go ahead with it!"

Mezruh tells him proudly, "We have obtained some gold using our currency! It's not very much, sir, but it will power the ship for a little while. We do have a small amount to be vaporized."

Zilog looks excited! He goes, "Very good, gentlemen! Return to the ship and let's evaluate the product."

After some crackle and static, Zilog hears Mezruh faintly say, "Orders received, sir. We're on our way."

The conversation ends, and Zilog turns back to his passenger acquaintances and excuses himself. He's got stuff to do.

But meanwhile, back at the jewelry store, Marjorie wants to know just how Lydia knows those very odd fellows who just left. Marjorie asks her, "You know those two weirdos?"

Lydia answers, "Not really, hun. We met them on the porch last night having coffee. Earl found them somewhere while he was out walking. You know Earl. He will talk to anyone who'll listen. But anyway, he brought them back to the home, right at coffee time. So that's where I know them from. They seem like okay guys. They said they were here visiting relatives."

Marjorie looks kind of nervous as she starts talking, "Lydia, those two nuts just bought 7,500 dollars' worth of gold rings and paid in cash!" Marjorie is getting excited and louder as she speaks, "I've never seen anything like it! And they wanted raw gold! It was weird!"

Lydia says, "You say they paid in cash?"

Marjorie goes on (she's still kind of rattled), "It's all in the safe! There's so much of it!"

Lydia looks shocked. She says, "They don't look rich." Marjorie says she can't believe how much money these guys had. And Lydia has some more to add. "Last night, an armored truck got stolen from outside the bank. I saw it on the news. Nobody saw who took it though. The guards went into the bank, and when they came out the truck was gone. The driver said it was locked up tight like always. And when they came back, it was gone. Whoever did this knows how to break into a vehicle fast! They haven't said how much money was in it yet."

Marjorie looks astonished. "Wow!" she says. "Do you think . . . those two old-timers stole an armored truck? They don't look the part for that kind of stuff. But they sure had a lot of money, and they sure were strange."

Back on the ship, Zilog is heading to the cargo area to open the door and wait for his comrades. As the door goes down, he sees passengers outside (that look like humans).

They are chatting and enjoying the sunshine and greenery. They too didn't have this back on Nibiru. So Zilog waves and walks down the ramp to visit with them. They are telling him how wonderful it is here and that they hope their new home is as beautiful. He assures them it is.

But he has to guide them away from the ramp because he is expecting two of his crewmembers to be back from a mission. Zilog tells them he's not sure what they'll be driving, but he expects them soon. And sure enough, a few minutes later, coming through the camouflage is a beat-up older-looking truck, with Mezruh and Orsello in it. As it stops, smoke gushes out from the underside. While the boys are getting out, smoke (stinky smoke) is wafting around.

Mezruh says, "I didn't want to pull it inside, sir. She's pretty smokey. I guess we should have got something a little better." Zilog isn't listening to Mezruh at all. He's looking at Orsello carrying a little bag.

"Ho-ho, what have we here?" Zilog says happily.

Orsello answers, "This is it, sir. It's not very much."

Zilog says, "Let's go inside and evaluate it further." The three go up the ramp and into the ship. Zilog leads the others to the propulsion room where there is a work table.

Orsello spills the jewelry bag onto the table, five little white boxes. He opens one as Zilog opens another. "You're right," Zilog says. "It's not very much." He takes the ring out of the box and examines it closer, holding it up to his face. He (Zilog) gathers the five rings and hands them to Mezruh. Zilog says, "Go ahead and process these. Get it in the tank, and we'll keep looking for more. But good work, gentlemen!"

CHAPTER 4

U P THE ROAD A LITTLE ways, Kornak is on his way back from his mission. He's excited about the information he has gathered. He's got some hot leads on gold and dogs!

He gets to the field with the new stand of trees, and he knows he's almost home. He starts to walk faster when he gets closer to the camouflage ring. As he passes through, he is surprised to see passengers (looking human) outside the ship, enjoying the outdoors. He didn't know about the commander authorizing people to be outside. But he sees the cargo ramp is down and everyone is calm and cheerful, so he assumes that everything is okay. He strides up that cargo ramp and through the cargo area. He's looking for his commander. Up the corridor to the helm he goes.

Zilog is in his seat in the control center. He's looking at a large computer screen with facts and data about gold sources on this planet. He is perplexed. It's not showing him much.

When all of a sudden, Kornak knocks on the doorframe (knock knock) and speaks, "Commander Zilog? Permission to enter, sir."

Zilog recognizes his nephew's voice. He spins his chair and sees Kornak as teenage human. "You look good in your disguise," he says, smiling. "Give me your report from the field!"

Kornak starts talking excitedly and too fast, "I've had a very productive day, sir! I found a place called a dog . . . dog . . . pound! That's it—dog pound."

Zilog's eyes light up! "Dogs!" he says. "How wonderful, corporal."

Kornak takes a deep breath and goes on, "Sir, there are so many different ones! Some are big, and some are small. Long fur, short fur, they're beautiful, sir. Oh, and they have different barks too." Zilog thinks back to Hiram's little bark and how much he misses him. But Kornak breaks him out of his sad mini flashback. Kornak's got more to talk about! He goes, "I talked to the lady at the place. I mean the dog pound, and she said they are thirty-five dollars each! Dogs, sir! Like corporal Slosser wanted. And it's right up the road, a little ways."

Kornak tries to keep talking, but Zilog interrupts him, "Very good, corporal. Settle down. Did you find me any gold?" Zilog wants to hear more about dogs, but he has to ask about gold, and he can't act ecstatic about the dog thing.

So Kornak comes back with his other big story—football! I mean gold. Yeah, gold, that's it. He starts rambling again, "Sir . . . um . . . yes and no on the gold thing."

Zilog looks intrigued and asks, "What? Elaborate please."

Kornak starts, "I found a group of people playing a game." Zilog rolls his eyes. Kornak goes on, still very excited, "They told me that the humans who play this game for a living compete to see which team is best at the game. And get this, sir. The winners get gold—big gold rings! I'm sure it would be enough to power us on to our new home! We just got to beat them at this game they play, and we get the gold! It's called football!"

Zilog looks very skeptical, saying, "How do we know this is all true? It sounds crazy, corporal."

Kornak responds (still excited), "All the people there were telling me about it. They all knew what it was. It's called the Super Bowl. All these famous football players get together and play the game until someone wins. And those guys get the gold rings, sir."

Zilog acts unimpressed, saying, "Super Bowl? Football? We don't know this game for one thing."

Kornak goes, "We can learn it. I'm learning it now, commander! If we can learn this game and then shape-shift into humans, we can beat them at their game and win the gold! And then go home, sir. What do you think?"

Zilog tells him, "See how hard this game is to learn. Meanwhile I'll be searching for gold in other ways. But stay on that, Kornak. Learn more about it. And good work with the dogazoids too."

Kornak responds, "Yes, sir. Thank you, sir." It seems like their (Zilog and Kornak's) relationship is mending.

In the morning, Kornak finds Adria in the cafeteria. She is sitting at a table with two female passengers, conversing while they eat. Kornak has important news for her. He knows she loves dogs and she had requested a search. And now Kornak has positive info, and she's gonna love it! He approaches and waits for a pause in their conversation. The women are wondering why he is standing there smiling, so they stop talking.

"Pardon me, ladies," he begins saying to all and then he turns to Adria and gives her the good news. "Adria, yesterday during my exploration, I found dogs! There are dogs here!"

Adria becomes ecstatic! She pumps her fists up high in the air and exclaims, "Yes! This is wonderful!" She is sooooo happy! "I was so hoping there were some here! Where did you find them, Kornak?"

He answers, "They aren't too far from here at all. It's walking distance." Adria can't wait to hear more. She's very excited. Kornak goes on, "They are all in one spot. It's a building with cages on the outside. The dogs are all friendly, and they all want to leave with you. It was so amazing." Adria is standing now, with her tray in hand, ready to go see the commander. She asks Kornak if he can take her to this place. "Of course!" Kornak says happily. She deposits her tray at the dishroom, and the two head for the exit. She needs to see Zilog to request permission to go on an exploration, to see dogs. Adria is trying to contain herself, but she is very excited. She has only seen dogs in pictures and video. This would be the first time she'll see them actually alive.

Kornak is excited just seeing her so pumped up. He's so glad that he could bring someone such happiness.

They find Zilog at the ship's helm (of course). He is in his captain's chair meditating with headphones on. He looks relaxed, maybe even napping. Kornak and Adria step in the doorway shushing each other, as they see him napping, (ahem) meditating. But he hears them shushing and jumps a little as he wakes. He takes off his headphones and sits up for conversation. He says, sounding cheerful, "Good morning, officers. How does this day find you?"

Adria speaks right up, "Good morning, commander. We're sorry to interrupt your meditation, sir." She's about to pop the question. "Sir," she says, "I've heard news that there are dogs here." She smiles at Kornak, and Zilog smiles too. She goes on excitedly, "Requesting permission to go and see and maybe arrange to obtain these animals, sir."

Zilog looks compliant. He knows how much this means to her. So he says to her, "Of course, Adria, but you must remember caution. You both have taken the form of these beings, but you have to act like them too. Don't give us away! All our lives depend on secrecy."

Then Zilog turns to Kornak to give him more instructions. He tells him, "Take some of the currency we have obtained and use it to trade for the animals. Make an honest deal and interact with these beings carefully. We don't know what to expect from them."

Kornak listens intently to Zilog's warnings and cautions, but inside he (Kornak) knows that these people are generally friendly and easy to get along with. The ones he has encountered so far have been very nice people.

As long as they stay disguised, no one will know they're aliens. There's no telling what these humans would do if they saw the aliens in their original reptilian form! They might freak out for sure. (Did we go over that?)

So anyway, after hearing Zilog's lecture, Kornak and Adria are off. They bring some currency from the canvas bags. Zilog also reminded Kornak to find out more about that game he had mentioned, the one with the gold at the end.

As they walk, Adria can't believe how wonderful this place is. The atmosphere is warm and sort of windy. And the greenery—trees, grass, birds! *It's beautiful,* she thinks. She has her crappy home planet to compare to.

So far their expedition has been pleasant. They've walked a ways, and they come to the neighborhood where Kornak was yesterday. He wants to show her where he met those kids, the ones who showed him football.

Adria is listening to him as he talks, but her mind is on dogs. She'll be patient and polite until this first part of the mission is over. Kornak walks her into this strange new world. She too is unfamiliar with these aboveground dwellings (houses). Cars with people in them going by. It all seems so amazing to her. She's never seen this before. *This planet is pretty neat,* she thinks. *It's so well preserved and unspoiled. Perhaps these beings aren't capable of destroying their atmosphere yet* (same thing Kornak thought). And white clouds roll by, looking fluffy! She loves it!

Kornak interrupts Adria's thoughts by saying, "There are some of the kids I played football with!" He points and says excitedly, "Over there!"

Adria looks to see a group of kids in a field. They are throwing something around, looks like a ball of some sort. *That must be a football!* she thinks.

Kornak is very happy he found his friends. And they remember him too, but as Mike. "Yo, Mike!" one yells. "Get over here!" Then they, all eight or nine of them, start toward Kornak and Adria, a herd of kids walking across a dusty field.

Kornak turns quickly to Adria and asks her, "What name do you want to be called?"

"Name?" Adria asks. "Um . . . how about Totzke?"

"What is it? Totzke?" Kornak asks as the others approach.

"Yes!" Adria says almost whispering. "It was my grandma's name."

Kornak says, "Okay, Totzke it is then."

He then turns to his friends to greet them and introduce them to his new friend. He remembers some of their names and a little of their slang from yesterday. He says loudly, "How are younz doing today? Tossin' the ball around a little?"

"Yup," one kid says. "Who's your friend, Mike?"

Mike says, "This is my sister, Totzke." Adria says hi to everyone and wonders about the sister thing.

Another kid says, "Let's pick up some teams! We got enough people to get a pretty good game going." So out on the field they go. Kornak is acting like he knows more about the game than he does. He's trying to impress Adria a little.

Before they get started, Kornak sees another kid coming to join the game. But he looks way too small to play with these bigger kids. The kids sure know him though! They all welcome him and call his name, Artie, as he approaches. All yell, "Hey, Artie, get out here! How're you doing? Where were you yesterday?"

Artie answers back in his little kid's voice, "I couldn't make it yesterday. Had stuff to do. My mom made me get a haircut."

Kornak asks one of the other kids if Artie plays this rough game with them. Lionel, whom Kornak met yesterday, tells him that Artie is their official. They call him first down Artie.

Lionel explains to Kornak that Artie marks off first downs and calls out Mississippis.

Kornak doesn't know what any of that means, but he nods his head yes like he does.

What Lionel means by counting Mississippis is that sometimes there aren't enough kids to have blockers on the line. So the defense has to count two or maybe three Mississippis before they can cross the line of scrimmage to rush the quarterback. Playing sandlot football almost always has someone counting Mississippis.

So anyway, when teams are picked, Mike and Totzke wind up on opposite sides. The other kids are helpful teaching them the game, although they can't believe that these two don't know anything about football. Kornak learned some yesterday, but he knows there is much more to it.

Adria is learning it quickly. She sees that it is rough and it gets loud too. She helps on several tackles. And she makes a catch and gets tackled herself. Her clothes are getting dirty, but that's okay. She's having fun, and she likes it!

And Artie is all attentive at his job, counting Mississippis at every snap of the ball and running downfield to mark first downs. He's very serious, exclaiming loudly "First down!" while pointing one arm stiffly toward the end zone. Adria thinks he is funny to watch, a cute little guy acting all serious.

Kornak is learning more about this game. He's getting better at it too, scoring one touchdown and making several other catches. When he makes the touchdown, the kids on his team go crazy celebrating. Mike and Totzke watch them with their chest bumps, high fives, and cheering. What a scene. Obviously scoring a touchdown is a big deal. Totzke laughs as Artie is running around with his arms straight up yelling "Hoo-hoo! Touchdown! Hoo-hoo! Touchdown!"

How fun this is. Our heroes are having a blast, with their new friends, playing this crazy game.

Back on the V-34, Zilog is contemplating his next move. He needs gold to get to the new planet. But this planet's gold is so coveted that it is hard to find and harder to obtain. Sending Mezruh and Orsello out on exploratory missions has been somewhat successful. But the amount of gold they brought back was minimal. Zilog appreciates his two officers risking their lives on these missions. They are dedicated and intelligent.

But he needs a better plan. Oh, sure he can send them out again, and he probably will. But he needs something different.

Zilog realizes that he has the kids, Kornak and Adria, out on a mission for dogs, which will be wonderful if and when it is successful. Zilog is a dog lover. Having another dog after all these years would be a miracle for him.

But he still has to come up with ways to get gold. He's pretty much ignoring Kornak's idea about some game where gold is passed out at the end. *That sounds crazy,* he thinks. So it's kind of off the list, for now anyway.

And wouldn't you know it, here come Mezruh and Orsello, and they're looking excited! Each has his own idea about getting more gold.

Mezruh starts, "Permission to enter, sir." Zilog replies, "Of course, gentlemen."

Orsello begins, "We've got some more ideas, sir."

Zilog's face takes on a cheerful look, and he exclaims loudly, "Well let's hear it! I'm open for suggestions. What have you got?" He sounds pretty pumped up.

Mezruh goes, "Well, sir, we've each got our own idea, so here's mine." Orsello gives him a dirty look for getting to go first. Mezruh keeps talking, "How about this, sir. We go back to that gold shop (he means jewelry shop), and we take 'em by surprise! We walk in there looking normal, and all of a sudden, we morph into big ugly monsters, scare the crap out of them, and grab all the gold that's in there. Then we jump into an escape vehicle and hightail it back here and get that stuff processing. And get this, sir. If they're chasing us, we can fire this thing up and take off with the fuel we have. Then we process the new gold while we're making our exit. What do you think, sir? We have to get aggressive here!"

Zilog responds with, "It sounds pretty desperate, Mezruh, and I realize we're in a bad situation. The plan is good especially with what we're learning about gold being hard to come by. These beings love it as jewelry, not fuel." Zilog surmises, "But let me put this idea on the list, Mezruh. It's a good idea."

Orsello chimes in, "That place doesn't have enough gold though, just little stuff."

Zilog then turns to Orsello and says, "Let's hear your idea."

Orsello starts talking in his raspy voice, "Okay, sir, how about this. We pick up the ship and move it someplace else where there is more gold to have. Maybe circle the planet with the fuel we have and look for more population than we have here. There's bound to be more gold where there's more beings."

Zilog looks very thoughtful as he responds, "Hmm, that's a good one too, but I feel it might be too risky. I think we'd be spotted as we were landing and maybe even attacked at that time. I'm sure there is more gold in heavily populated areas, but it is very risky to move this thing around."

Orsello replies, "But, sir, we've got this new camouflage thing that hides the ship."

Zilog responds, "It still sounds crazy, Orsello. They'll see a giant cloud landing? Not very believable. I think the ship is better off staying here. If we have to travel to find bigger cities, then we'll do that by using the vehicles that are here. The vehicles on this planet seem rather easy to come by. Am I right, gentlemen?" Both nod in agreement. Zilog goes on, "So that sounds like the way to go. If we have to travel to obtain gold, then we will. We're getting better at this. But, guys, don't take that smoking truck that you pulled up in. It looks pretty tired. Get something newer. And we don't know what their vehicles run on fuel-wise, but we'll have to learn that too. So, my faithful comrades, be off with you." Zilog tells them, "Go and seek the fuel we require to complete this mission. Try not to use force if you can help it. Take some currency with you, but don't look flashy with it. Try not to intermingle with these beings. They are dangerous." Zilog is rambling a bit. He goes on, "Good luck, gentlemen. Please return safely even if unsuccessful. I need you, and I care greatly for you both. Be careful."

And with that Mezruh and Orsello each shake hands with their commander as though they will never see him again. Then, they all head out of the helm and down the corridor to the cargo area. Mezruh and Orsello don't seem afraid at all. They are hardened military to the bone.

Anyway, they all go through the cargo area and down the big ramp, chatting a little as they go. It's a nice warm day outside. They get to the old truck they borrowed yesterday, and Mezruh and Orsello jump on in. Zilog doesn't, but he stands at the door to give more instructions (as he always does). He tells them, "Now make sure you trade this thing in. If you're going far away, this is not the ride for you!"

"Yes, sir!" comes from both of them at the same time.

Mezruh fires the old bomb up. Smoke immediately comes out from under the hood. (Oil is leaking from the valve covers onto the exhaust manifolds causing massive smoke.) Zilog steps back quickly waving his hand in front of his face. He breaks into a laugh and asks, "Where did you get this thing?"

Mezruh tells him, "It was sitting outside a junkyard!" All three laugh, and the two heroes pull out to have a new adventure, no telling how this one will turn out. Our boys have aggression on their minds.

Orsello asks Mezruh, "Did he say we could morph into monsters and go crazy on our victims?" He's smiling and rubbing his hands together.

Mezruh smiles and says, "I'm not sure he said to do all that, but if we have to, we will."

So they take the old truck near where they ditched the armored truck and leave the smokey old thing there. Out walking they go, looking for something better to drive. They're coming up on the feedstore again—same old feedstore. There are not too many good-looking cars parked outside. So they keep going, and up the road a ways they find a worthy-looking vehicle. It's a fairly new Chevrolet truck, parked outside a house with no one in it or around it. So the guys make their move. Shhhh . . . Mezruh unlocks the driver door with his shape-shifting fingers, and he's in in a jiffy. He works the power locks on the door until one opens the passenger door, and Orsello is in too! And vroom! It starts right up with a twist of the ignition finger. And they're off! Mezruh has learned how to do the shifter pretty good too. He doesn't know that not all vehicles are automatics. But the ones he's tried so far were, luckily. If they had tried a vehicle that had a manual transmission, it would have been a lot harder to learn. Automatics are pretty easy to master, which is good for our heroes.

So they get this cool Chevro going, and they're both smiling. Orsello asks, "Do you want to take this back to the ship and show Zilog? He'll like this thing. It's nice." Then he starts messing with the knobs on the dashboard. He gets the air conditioner blowing full blast! Both guys laugh as they hold their hands up in front of the vents. Soon that novelty wears off, and they just drive quietly.

Then Mezruh says, "I don't think it's a good idea to go back to the ship. Zilog might think we're just playing around. Let's go on with our mission. He'll see this thing when we get back."

Orsello nods in agreement. Then he starts messing with the other gadgets on the dashboard. Suddenly loud classic rock n' roll music blasts out from somewhere. It's Van Halen's "Ice Cream Man." Orsello says, "What cool music these humans have." Both guys are surprised, but they like it. So now they have a decent vehicle, air conditioner blasting and some cool music playing.

They're not sure where they are going, but they're on their way! Orsello calls Zilog to let him know of their success. Orsello speaks, "Red calling blue, red to blue over."

Once again Zilog is outside when the call comes in. He holds his hand to his face and turns toward the woods and speaks, "This is blue. Come in, red. Over."

Orsello begins, "Commander Zilog, this is Orsello."

Zilog answers, "What have you got?"

"We've got a vehicle, sir. It's newer and nicer."

"I'm glad to hear it! Do you think it will travel a ways?"

"Yes, sir!" He sounds excited. "It's cold in here, and it plays music." Then a brainstorm idea comes to Orsello. He looks at Mezruh while talking to Zilog to see if Mezruh is going to approve of his idea. He goes on talking to Zilog, "Do you think it would be okay if we brought this thing back to the ship and installed a power booster on it? We might need one to make our escape."

Zilog replies, "I don't think we have one of those on board."

Orsello says, "Yes, sir, we do. It's on the utility vehicle."

"Are you sure we can install it on the vehicle you have?"

"Yes, sir! Anything with wheels will work. We can adapt, sir."

Zilog agrees, "Alright then, get back here with it."

"Orders received, commander. Over and out."

Mezruh speaks, "That's a good idea, big O! Let's power this thing up!"

So they head back to the ship, and it only takes a few minutes to pull the power booster off the utility vehicle. These guys are excellent mechanics. They put the loose parts into the back of the Chevy and say their goodbyes once again. Only now a lot of passengers are standing around wishing them well. It's a very heartfelt moment.

So the boys pull out kind of teary eyed after all the goodbyes. Soon though, their newfound love comes back—music, jamming music! Up goes the volume! It plays Bob Seger's "Ramblin' Gamblin' Man." Yeah! Good song!

I'm gonna tell my tale. C'mon . . . c'mon! Ha! Give a listen!

As they go, they come to an interstate highway and proceed to get on. Mezruh follows the other drivers who look like they know where they're going. Up the ramp they go. Mezruh notices that other drivers are going much faster now. One guy honks at them. *Jerk,* Mezruh thought. But then he steps on it to speed up. They are cruising now! Loud rock music is blasting. It's Molly Hatchet's "Bounty hunter" this time. Wooo!

Did you know five hundred dollars will get your head blown off? It will. Ha ha ha (Danny Joe Brown on vocals).

Back at the neighboorhood field, Kornak and Adria are having a blast playing football. They are getting to know their friends better. They're learning about the game too—line of scrimmage, end zones, first downs. Adria or Totzke is taking it all in. She's not sure if she's ever going to need this information again, but she's having fun with it. During one huddle, she asks a few questions about the Super Bowl. It gets everybody going! She asks the kid next to her, "So this Super Bowl thing sounds like a pretty big deal, ay?"

The kid she's talking to is Wes, and he starts explaining more details about it. He says, "It happens once a year. The two best teams in the NFL play to see who is the best."

The other kids are adding stuff too. "It happens in two weeks," one kid says.

"This year, it's in Washington," another says. "They usually have it in warm climate cities." All the kids are talking now.

Adria laughs with delight as she gets flooded with information, and then she slips in a question, "What about those rings?"

Wes answers that one excitedly, "Big fat gold ones! The losers get smaller ones, but the winners get the big ones."

"And they're made of gold, you say?"

"Oh, yes," Wes tells her. "With diamond clusters. Why are you asking about the rings?"

Adria looks embarrassed and says, "I don't know. I guess I just like jewelry." (She dodges that one.)

So they call the next play and break the huddle, and the game resumes. Totzke lines up behind Wes in the fullback slot. He calls some signals and takes the snap and hands off to her—fullback up the middle, for a gain of about six yards. It's not bad, kind of rough tackle though.

Everyone's adrenaline is pumping. The game is getting rougher as it goes. All the kids' clothes are dirty. Some are torn. No one cares though. They're into this game!

Kornak and Adria can see that these kids are getting mad at each other. They're all very competitive, and sometimes tempers flare. Hey, it happens. And in the middle of some name calling and angry words, here comes another new addition to the group. It's a girl, a blond-headed girl. She's bigger than Artie, but not as big as the rest of the kids. Her name is Jodee, and she's about eight or so. She's pushing a kid's grocery cart, a brightly colored plastic grocery cart, green and yellow. And Jodee's got a bunch of cool stuff in it too.

Kornak and Adria (Mike and Totzke) are standing next to each other watching the other kids argue about the football game. They also see this little girl coming with her grocery cart. The other kids haven't noticed her until she is right among them. Wes sees her first and goes from mad to happy. He says, "Hey, guys, Jodee's here!

And she brought Disc War!" Everyone stops arguing and turns happily toward Jodee and her cart of stuff. They all know her. She is one of them. She's Wes's little sister. And that stuff she has in her cart is a game they all invented. It's called "Disc War."

It's a pretty cool game they came up with. It consists of a Frisbee, eight small orange cones, and two sets of flip numbers to keep score—pretty basic stuff. She also has a boom box radio with fresh batteries, for jamming. The kids crowd around Jodee's cart, and all agree that they'll take a break from football and play some Disc War.

It's amazing how creative kids are. They came up with this game right here on this field.

Our heroes Mike and Totzke watch as the cones are set up. And the flip numbers are out too.

Jodee's cart is now empty except for the radio. She pushes the cart over to the sideline, out of the way of the game.

The kids know to split into two teams. The disc (Frisbee) is being tossed around too, just warming up. The teams will be competing against each other (duh). The objective is to cause the other team to drop the disc instead of making a catch. When one team drops the disc, the other team gets a point (sort of like volleyball).

Mike and Totzke again go on opposite teams. Mike learns this new game from the kids on his team, as does Totzke from her teammates.

Lionel explains to Mike, "You gotta get up there and throw this thing." He stops and asks, holding up the disc, "You ever seen one of these?"

Mike instantly says, "No."

Lionel rolls his eyes and continues, "You throw this disc at them as hard as you can. You want them to drop it. So throw it crazy. Throw it hard, Mike!" Lionel demonstrates by throwing the disc hard and straight at a kid on the other team. The kid flubs the catch, and the disc falls to the ground. Lionel pumps his hands in the air and proclaims loudly, "Yes! That's what I mean right there!" He turns to Mike and says, "See, Mike? You gotta get them to drop it!"

Mike nods yes and says, "I see. I think I've got it. Get them to drop it."

Lionel goes on, "When they drop it, we get a point." He points at the flip numbers and says, "And when our side drops it, they get a point. Copish, Mike?" Mike nods his head yes, acting confident. Lionel goes on, "And if it comes your way, Mike, don't drop it!"

Now Kornak and Adria have never thrown a disc before. They are watching to see how it goes. They can't help thinking that it looks like their ship zooming around. But that's a secret.

(Ssshh.)

You sort of curl your arm around it in front of your body, Kornak thinks as he observes someone throwing it, *and you whip it, until your arm is stretched out in front of you.*

Meanwhile, Adria is learning differently over on the other team. Jodee is showing her how to throw it behind the back style. Jodee explains to her, "You sort of lean to the side and pull the disc behind your back." She demonstrates awkwardly. "And you just let it fly!" She doesn't throw it though. She hands it to Totzke and says, "Try it. You want to make those guys drop it."

Totzke feels a little silly with this new idea. She leans like Jodee showed her, pulls the disc behind her back, and lets it rip! She giggles as she throws it, but still the disc flies pretty well. It flies straight and then veering left, and someone on the other team catches it. Totzke seems to have it though.

"Okay!" Wes yells out. "Let's play! Crank up the radio, Jodee!" Jodee jogs over to her cart where the radio is and turns it on. She's got it set on a bubblegum pop station. That's her kind of music— Bruno Mars's "Uptown Funk."

> Saturday night we'll be hittin the spot.
> Don't believe me just watch!

So the game starts. The disc is volleyed back and forth, both sides trying to get the other side to drop it. There's a space between the two teams of about fifty feet. Each team has a front line that they serve from. It's pretty well-thought-out. The cones mark the side boundaries, as well as the front lines.

Also, another aspect of the game is that each kid has a unique way of throwing the disc.

And everybody knows each other's throws too. The older kids' throws are more threatening, because they throw harder. But still everyone is honing their skills with some crazy ways to throw the disc. One of the bigger kids has a throw where he throws it way up in the sky toward the sun, so it comes diving down at the other team with the sun behind it. It's very hard to catch. He has that throw down! Another kid taught himself to throw the disc upside down. So it flies all wobbly, also hard to catch. Then there's the straight hard throw right at the other team's front line. The lower, the better, so it's just over the line, in bounds. It's hard to catch.

So anyway, the serve rotates in this game, also like volleyball, and now it's Mike's turn to serve that bad boy. He steps up to the line, still unsure how this is gonna go. He cocks the disc by curling it across his body, like he had seen the others doing. And he lets it fly! The other kids laugh a little as the disc curves to the right and goes out of bounds.

"Bad toss," Wes says with a slight chuckle.

Again, the kids can't believe that these two newcomers don't know how to do this either.

First, they were totally unfamiliar with the game of football. Now they've never thrown or seen a flying disc before. It's kind of suspicious.

"You'll get better at it, Mike!" Wes assures him. "Practice and repetition will get you there, bro."

Mike looks embarrassed, kicking dirt around. But everyone is forgiving, and the game moves on quickly. It's sort of like at a karaoke setting, when someone sings terrible but the crowd applauds with sympathetic support. It's sort of like that.

The other team serves back, and it flies over Kornak's head so fast he couldn't get his hands up in time to catch it. Luckily one of his teammates is in place behind him and makes the catch. But Kornak should have had it though. His teammates know it. He bends over and puts his hands on his knees, to catch his breath. Kornak thinks to himself, *I've got to get better at this.* Now it's Totzke's turn to serve the disc. She steps confidently up to the cone-marked line and pulls the disc behind her back like Jodee showed her. She whips it good, and the disc goes straight. It's not bad for her first try, but alas someone on the other team catches it. So no point is scored for her.

But the aliens are learning this game pretty fast. Kornak thinks to himself as the game goes on that learning this game isn't really part of their mission. Although it's fun and everyone is enjoying it, it's not really on the agenda. Just then the disc whizzes by him, and he misses another chance to make a catch, because he wasn't paying attention. The other team gets a point, and Mike's teammates are disappointed that he let one get by. A few snide remarks are mumbled. Mike apologizes and swears he'll get better at this, and his teammates relent.

So the game goes on. Back and forth goes the disc, and the points add up as catches are dropped by both sides. It's Adria's turn to serve, and she does. But the wind catches it, and the disc floats over into the yard where the big mean dog lives. Kornak was hoping this wouldn't happen. He knows how emotional Adria is about dogs, but this one is a bad example.

And here he comes now, barking and looking mean. Adria is amazed as she stares at the menacing creature. She puts her hands over her mouth and cries softly. She's never seen one before! Ever! She can't believe her eyes.

Lionel goes into the yard to retrieve the disc. The big dog is okay with him being in the yard, but he barks at the other kids standing around the fence. Mike watches Totzke closely as she walks to the fence, weaving between the kids to get closer to the dog. Mike moves to block her from the animal, not knowing if it will attack or not. He certainly doesn't want Totzke to get injured or worse by this thing.

Lionel gets it calmed down enough to pet. He sees that Totzke seems very interested in his dog. So he tells her the dog's name is Bufo. Totzke is amazed as she reaches over the fence to pet him. The dog allows her to pet his head, but he is still not friendly. Lionel tells her, "My dad doesn't want me bringing my friends around Bufo. He might bite. He's a watchdog." Totzke is still amazed, petting Bufo's head gently.

Mike tells her, "Let's move along now, hon. Leave the man's dog alone."

The other kids have taken notice of what a heartfelt moment this is for Totzke. One girl mumbles, "She's getting all emotional over petting Lionel's mean ass dog? What's up with that?"

Another girl asks sarcastically, "Never seen a dog before?" Totzke turns to her and says very seriously, "No, I haven't!"

The other kids stare in disbelief. One kid goes, "She's never seen a dog before? Come on! No way!"

Mike chimes in, "She means . . . um . . . a dog this big. Yeah, that's it."

Totzke agrees, as she wipes tears away, "Yes, I meant a dog this big."

Mike puts his arm around Totzke and turns her away from the dog. They all start back to the field to resume play. Mike can tell that Totzke isn't over the moment. She is shaking slightly and talking much softer than before. Her eyes have a fixed stare, and she seems to be in shock.

She says to Mike, "I'd like to see the other ones. Can we go now?" Kornak agrees of course.

He wants to get her out of this very emotional moment and away from the kids. They are inquisitive. They wonder why these two strange people have so few life experiences.

No football? No Frisbee? And the one girl (Totzke) seems like she's never seen a dog before?

They were strange alright. But kids are very accepting. And in their world, everyone is welcome, even weirdos.

"You guys are leaving?" Wes yells to them as they are walking away. "Don't say goodbye or nothing?"

Mike says back loudly because of distance, "She's not feeling well, guys. We're going to move on, but it was fun!"

Then Totzke turns and adds, "Yeah, guys, thanks! It was fun!"

All the kids wave and say goodbye pleasantly. Then they get on with their game. Kornak and Adria proceed back through the neighborhood to the main road. Kornak knows where to go from here, and he knows it's not very far. He speaks to her, "We go this way (pointing) to that light way up there." He uses his newfound knowledge to impress Adria. "Then you hang a right." He says motioning with his arm excitedly. "And then we're there. You'll see them! Lots of 'em, Adria, you're gonna love this! And the beings are nice too. Hopefully we can come home with some dogs today!" Kornak is excited now. He's trying to get her pumped up some too. She seems kind of down still from the previous encounter (with Bufo and the kids making fun of her). So Kornak is trying to cheer her up, as they get closer to her next emotional breakdown.

CHAPTER 5

OUR OTHER TWO HEROES, ON a mission seeking gold, are stuck in a traffic jam. It's rush hour at 5:30 p.m., bumper to bumper on I-95. Mezruh and Orsello are feeling paranoid. Cars are all around, some honking their horns. Luckily the air conditioner works well in their latest vehicle—and the radio!

Thank goodness for music in this boring stop-and-go mess. Right now on the radio is REO Speedwagon's "Keep Pushin'." It's a good song cranked up loud!

I used to be lonely, till I learned about living alone. I found other things to keep my mind on.

But our guys feel like other people are looking at them, for no reason though. They fit in just fine, a couple of old guys in a Chevy truck, playing loud rock music. Maybe it's a little weird.

Eventually the traffic jam clears up, and all vehicles resume normal speed. At this point, in between songs on the radio, there's a strange noise. It's going "Bong, bong, bong!" The boys aren't sure what's making this sound, but it's not the radio. (It's the low fuel alarm. Not all vehicles have it, but Chevy trucks do.) "Bong, bong, bong," it goes on. The next song starts on the radio, but Orsello turns it down to keep figuring out what's bonging. Mezruh notices that next to the fuel gauge on the dash there is a little yellow light that is blinking off and on in beat with the "Bong, bong, bong." So they figure out this thing must need fuel!

Mezruh grabs the next exit, using his blinker like a pro. His driving is getting much better as he learns from other cars around him. He's learning about stop lights too. Red means stop, green means go, and yellow means slam on the brakes!

There is a lot of hustle and bustle at the intersection where they get off the highway. There are two convenient store gas stations and one strip plaza. There's a closed-down restaurant in front of the strip plaza.

The boys are deciding where to fuel up. Mezruh says, "The easiest one to get to is this one right here," as he pulls into a Chevron station on the right.

Orsello agrees saying, "This one it is then!" He seems excited about another adventure starting.

Mezruh sees other cars and trucks at what he assumes are the pumps. So he cautiously pulls up to a pump and cuts the engine off with his ignition finger. Then they agree to sit there a few minutes and observe how other drivers are fueling their vehicles. Hmmm.

They observe a human guy coming out of the store. He goes up to the car in front of theirs and pulls the nozzle out of the pump, as the aliens watch intently. Then with his other hand, the guy opens a little hatch door on the side of his car and unscrews something and puts the nozzle in the hole. He squeezes a trigger on the nozzle and stands frozen like that for a minute or so. After that, the man puts the nozzle back in its place on the pump, screws on his gas cap, and closes the little door. Mission accomplished, he gets in his car and leaves. Our boys look at each other and agree this can be done. It didn't look very hard.

Orsello says, "I'll go in to exchange currency. Do you want to stay here and work the pump?"

"Sure," Mezruh answers, "I've got to find that hatch door." He opens the door and starts getting out, still talking, "You go explore and have your currency ready." Orsello gets out of the truck and comes around to the driver side to help look for the gas door. He also wants to check out the nozzle and fuel pump in general. They both stand there gawking around a few seconds, and then Mezruh says, "You going in? You want me to go?"

Orsello barks back at him, "No! I'm going. I'm going! I just wanted to help you and check all this stuff out." (He waves his hand around.)

Mezruh looks annoyed, saying, "Well you seen it. Now get!" (He points to the store.)

Two old guys having a little disagreement at the fuel pump—it's no big deal.

So Orsello heads for the door pulling out his wad of cash as he walks. He peels off a fifty and goes inside. As he gets in, he sees that there is a line of people waiting to give their money. One guy in line has a big colorful box in his hand (beer). A lady has her purse hanging on her arm, but she has her billfold in her hand ready to make a transaction. Orsello observes these things as he falls into line and waits patiently. He is amused at how this store is so well stocked with products. *There's stuff everywhere,* he thinks to himself as he looks around. He's standing next to a rack with beef jerky and cashews and other stuff like that. He doesn't know what any of it is, but he decides to buy some of it. He also grabs a Reese's from the wall of candy behind the jerky rack. What the heck.

Just then, two guys come in and get in line behind our man. These younger guys are talking too. They're having a rather loud conversation as they wait in line. Orsello listens in.

One guy (Tony) says, "They ain't gonna be able to pull it off. I'm telling you right now! Peyton ain't got nothing left. You know I'm right, homey!"

The other guy (Steve) answers, "I know you're wrong, bro-daddy! He's still got that long ball. Peyton ain't done yet. And on top of that, Denver's D is lightning fast. They got to Brady all day!"

"Yeah maybe so, homey," Tony argues back. "But the cats are a different team than the pats. Big Cam is a lot younger and more athletic than Tom. Besides, Brady has been on top for a long time. It's time for a new sheriff."

Orsello listens intently. He doesn't know what they're talking about, but as serious as they sound, whoever they're talking about must be leaders of some kind. He listens on.

Tony says, "We'll see, Steve-a-reno. Your Broncos are gonna fold up like a cheap suit. Ha!" He says this as he puts Steve in a headlock, horseplaying around.

Steve tells him, "Get off me, man! You're wrinkling up my jacket, punk! I'm telling your mother."

"Leave my mom outta this." Tony lets go the headlock and says, "Hey, where we watching it at your house or mine? How about yours? Your TV is better than mine."

"Yeah, yours ain't been right since your kids pulled it off the table that time. The picture's kind of fuzzy and off-center. That's distracting, bro. It's hard to follow when my team is kicking your team's ass!" Steve now puts Tony in a headlock.

Orsello chuckles a bit as this play fight goes on behind him. He thinks to himself, *These humans seem okay, with their loud talk and play wrestling, not quite as intimidating as Commander Zilog presumes.*

Now the line is gone, and it is Orsello's turn to buy his stuff. He's kind of nervous as he puts his purchases on the counter. The girl cashier rings him up cheerfully. "Will this be all, sir?" she asks.

Orsello answers, "These and some fuel for my machine out there." "Okay!" she says. "These come to 9.88." She holds up the bag of honey-roasted cashews and says to him, "These are so good!" He only grunts in response as she bags up his stuff. "Okay, sir, which machine are you in?" she asks as she turns to look outside at the fuel pumps.

"The brown truck, with the old guy standing there." (He doesn't know the make of the truck.)

"The brown Chevy truck?" she asks.

"Yeah, that's it. Can I have the rest of this (he hands her the fifty) in fuel please?"

"So you want 40.12 in fuel on pump 7," she says, still very cheerful.

"Yes, please," Orsello responds. He's trying to keep it brief, so this girl doesn't get suspicious of him. He's very paranoid, being on a strange planet such as this.

But the girl asks him one more question as he's picking up his bag of stuff, startling him, "Would you like a receipt, sir?" (He thought the deal was over.)

"Umm . . . no, thanks," he tells her, not knowing what a receipt even is. He hopes it wasn't important.

So he heads for the door as the two guys who are behind him are still play fighting and talking loud. *What a couple of nuts,* he thinks to himself. *This planet is alright.*

As Orsello gets back to the truck, he sees that Mezruh has the nozzle in the hole ready to go.

While his buddy was in the store paying, Mezruh was watching other people fueling their cars. He's seen that you pull the nozzle out of the holder on the pump and you push a big button that says 87 on it. There are other buttons, but everyone uses the 87 button (octane). Orsello is impressed with his partner's watchful eye. Mezruh holds the trigger squeezed, pumping fuel. He can feel the cold fuel rushing through the handle. Forty dollars' worth only takes a few minutes or so to pump. He puts the nozzle back in its place on the pump, and they are ready to go! Nothing to it.

As they get in the truck, Orsello notices the two guys from inside the store are coming out, still clowning around but now they have a plastic football they just bought at the register.

Steve cocks it back and says, "Go long!" Tony takes off running toward their car at the fuel pump. Mezruh and Orsello are getting a kick out of these two entertaining characters.

So Steve floats a pass, but it's a terrible pass that bounces on the ground as Tony stops running. "What kind of crap was that?" he asks loudly. "You ain't on my team!"

Steve fires back, "Give me a break, man! I'm not warmed up or nothing. I can do better than that."

Tony picks up the ball and throws a perfect strike back to Steve.

Tony says with enthusiasm, "Now that's a pass! I still got it!" Steve agrees with him, saying, "Yeah, you do."

Our guys pull away from the gas station giving the younger dudes a friendly wave.

"What a couple of clowns," Orsello says. "This planet is a crazy place! So far, they don't seem too hostile."

"I know," Mezruh says. "Everyone here seems happy. I haven't seen any nuclear devices flying around either. Sooo . . ." Mezruh says to his buddy, "what's in that bag you have?" He points at it on the seat. "What'cha got? You bought something in there, didn't ya?" he asks.

Orsello perks up and picks up the bag. "Oh yeah, I forgot all about it! I was standing there in line, and all this stuff was next to me, so I figured 'What the heck! Let's check some of it out.'" As he is pulling the three products out of the bag, he says, "I'm pretty sure it's all food." He holds up the honey-roasted cashews and says, "The girl said these are really good." Mezruh is looking over at the stuff as he drives. He seems interested. Orsello tears open the cashews awkwardly. Some of them spill all on his lap and the seat. They both laugh as Orsello pours some into his hand and then some into Mezruh's outstretched hand. He wants some too! Crunch, crunch, crunch!

They both love them. Orsello says with his mouth full, "She was right! These are good."

Mezruh, also with his mouth full, says, "Who? A girl you say?" "Yes, the one who sold them to me. She was pretty," Orsello says

kind of dreamy, like he's in love or something.

Mezruh takes on a look of anger and scolds his buddy, "You were supposed to go in there and pay for fuel, not become attracted to one of the females here."

Orsello just rolls his eyes. "Yeah, yeah, yeah," he says. "It wasn't anything like that, bro. She was just a nice girl. Chatty, you know? I didn't talk too much."

Mezruh lightens up some saying, "Okay then, keep it that way." He reaches over and punches Orsello on the shoulder lightly, like friends do. They both laugh a little and continue scarfing down the cashews. The cashews don't stand a chance.

As they pull out of the gas station, they're contemplating what to do next.

Orsello says, "So do you want to get back on the big road or hang around here a while?"

Mezruh answers him with, "Why don't we look for something to eat? I'm hungry! Those nuts were good but not enough."

Orsello goes, "Eat it is then."

Mezruh smiles saying, "We did the fuel thing pretty well. Let's see how they eat on this planet!"

So the boys drive on a bit looking for a place that might have something to eat. "Hmm . . . Travelodge, Mini-storage, Walmart." Orsello points up ahead. "What's that one, with the big yellow M in the front? The place looks pretty busy."

"Yes, it does, bro," Mezruh says excitedly. "Let's check it out. I bet it's a food port." (That's what they call it.) So Mezruh turns on his right blinker and swings the truck right on in. The parking lot is crowded with cars and people walking about.

It looks kind of intimidating to the guys. Mezruh spots the drive-thru line that curls around the back. He jumps in the line hoping they won't have to exit the vehicle. The aliens are both observing the cars ahead to see what they have to do here to get some food. As they get closer to the colorful readerboard, Mezruh hangs his head about half out the window so he can hear the guy in front of them as he is ordering. The guy says to the readerboard, "Ah yeah, give me, um . . . two of the number 3s with a Pepsi and a Diet Coke. And gimme two Quarter Pounders with that too. That's all."

The wall says back, "Please pull to the first window, sir." So that guy pulls forward, and so does Mezruh. Now they're at the readerboard, and it sure is big! There are lots of pictures of food. He and Orsello gaze at all the stuff McDonald's has. But Mezruh, without asking Orsello what he wants, just starts talking, "Ah yeah, give me, um . . . two of the number 3s with a Pepsi and a Diet Coke, and throw on a couple of Quarter Pounders with that too" (same as the last guy ordered).

Orsello says, not knowing at all what any of it is, "That'll will do."

The wall instructs them to pull forward. As they stop at the first window, Mezruh pulls a fifty out of his pocket and gets ready to deal. The girl at the window says, "That will be 17.88, sir, and did you know that your order was exactly the same as the car in front of you?"

Mezruh shrugs his shoulders and says sarcastically while handing her the crisp fifty, "Wow, that's amazing."

(It seems our boys aren't that good at being friendly. They would rather be gruff and standoffish.)

So anyway, the girl reaches out with his change and counts it into his hand pleasantly. "Thirty-two dollars and twenty-two cents, sir."

Mezruh takes the cash but is unsure what to do with it. So he hands it to Orsello. Then the girl instructs him to pull forward to the next window. He sees that the car in front of them is at the next window, and they are receiving their food, in white bags. He observes that no more currency is being called for. Then that car pulls away, and Mezruh pulls on up. The little sliding window opens, and Mezruh is taken aback as the girl says hello to them. This female human has dark skin. The guys were unaware that these humans have different colors. Their race (Anunnaki) doesn't have different colors. All are greenish gray. So the pretty black chick catches them both by surprise. She hands them the food and drinks in their cardboard holder and then the bags of food.

"Would you guys like some extra ketchup?" Her voice is soft and mesmerizing.

Mezruh likes it, and he sits there staring for a moment. He turns his head sideways as though in disbelief. *This being is so beautiful,* he thinks. Then he snaps out of it and answers her question. "Ketchup?" he repeats. "Sure, give me some ketchup!" (He doesn't know what it is, but what the heck.) He wants to keep talking to this girl. She turns back around with the ketchup packets and hands them to him in a wad. She has ornate gold on her hands and long colorful fingernails. Mezruh notices all of this of course as he puts both hands out the window to receive the packets and she puts them in his cupped hands. Several of the packets fall to the ground, and the girl giggles about it. Mezruh now notices her pretty smile and her laugh. He giggles with her.

"No big deal, sir," she says as she pulls her hand away. Her perfume scent wafts lightly into the truck. "Have a nice day, you guys." Mezruh pulls his ketchup packets into the truck as the girl closes her little window. Transaction is over. Mezruh is sorry it ended so abruptly. He wants to talk to her some more.

Orsello turns to him and starts in, saying, "Pull forward, Mezruh. What are ya falling in love or something?" He chuckles a little and slaps him on the arm. Mezruh gives him an angry look, throws the ketchup on the seat, and pulls away from the window. He sure wants to talk to that girl some more though! It seems like both of these two are taking notice of the female beings on this planet! The boss said not to though.

So they pull away from the drive-thru window and park so they can eat. The smell of McDonald's food fills the truck. And boy it smells good. Orsello pulls out a Quarter Pounder still in the box and goes to take a bite. Mezruh reaches up quickly to stop him. "No, no, no!" he tells him. "You don't eat that part!" Mezruh takes the little box out of Orsello's hand and shows him how to open it, revealing the hamburger inside. He takes it out of the box and holds it up handing it to Orsello saying, "This is what you eat." He holds up the box and says, "Not this!" He throws it to the floor.

Taking the burger, Orsello says, "Thanks, homey!" And he takes a big bite.

Mezruh looks confused and asks him, "What did you call me?"

Orsello now talking with his mouth full says, "Homey. It's what they say here. I heard those two guys at the fuel station talking, and they called each other homey. So I thought I'd use it on ya."

Mezruh, also with his mouth full, says, "Homey? I wonder where they get that."

Orsello answers, "I don't know, but if everyone here is like those two, then this would be an ideal living environment. Beings who all get along with each other? Maybe Zilog was wrong about this being a dangerous warring place."

So anyway, they scarf down all the food like starving animals and decide they want more.

Vroom goes the engine, and back through the drive thru they go again! They have the same exact order as before. Mezruh has it memorized—two number 3s, Pepsi, Diet Coke, two Quarter Pounders, 17.88 all that. The girl at the first window seems kind of suspicious but still friendly. She thinks to herself, *These guys were just here a little while ago ordering the same exact thing, which also (she remembers) was the same thing that the car in front of him had ordered. How crazy is that! He's probably going to pay with another brand-new fifty-dollar bill too.*

And sure as rain, Mezruh pulls out another brand-new bill to pay with. They have the change from the last transaction lying on the seat, but they don't know how to use it. Besides, these others work fine (the fifties). They don't realize they're leaving a trail bigger than . . . well . . . you know. Those stolen bills have numbers on them. Our guys don't know that though. The first window girl changes another fifty for them cheerfully, but you can bet she's making a mental note of all this.

Pulling up to the second window, Mezruh is disappointed that the dark-skinned female human he liked wasn't there anymore. It is instead a male adolescent human, light skinned and not the same. The kid gives them their food, but to Mezruh it just isn't as good. When the kid asks him if he wants extra ketchup, he looks down sadly and says, "No, thanks." It's not the same at all.

So as Mezruh gets over his broken heart, he pulls the truck into another parking spot and shuts it off. It's time to chow down some more. This food is sooooo much better than the manna food back on the ship. Burgers and fries are the bomb! And these carbonated drinks are very amusing also. Mezruh takes a big slug off his Pepsi, and after a few moments, he lets out a big ole burp! Both of them laugh. They've never experienced this before. They don't have this kind of drink on their planet. Orsello does it too. He takes a big drink from his straw and boom! A giant buuurrrppp comes out. "That was a good one," he proudly proclaims, as they both laugh. This place is so crazy!

So they gobble up most of the second batch of food, and now they are full (finally).

Bags and wrappers litter the truck's interior. Sleepiness is creeping up on them. The boys don't know anything about hotels, so they just agree to sleep in the truck, in the parking lot at McDonald's. Mezruh goes ahead and moves the truck to a further away spot and backs it in. Now they can observe these beings in their natural habitat, the parking lot at Mickey D's. As they sit in the truck observing, they see that these beings all carry handheld devices of different sizes and shapes (phones). They are either holding the devices next to their head or in front of their face.

Mezruh says to his buddy, "These beings seem to be very dependent on . . . whatever those things are."

Orsello agrees saying, "Almost all of them have one. Looks like an addiction to me. It's got to be a communication device, perhaps an ancient version of the ones we have implanted in our hands."

Mezruh agrees, sounding kind of groggy, "Yup, I think you're right." He lets out a yawn and says, "I think I need to sleep a while."

"I'm with ya, homey," Orsello says as he leans his head to the window. Out they go. They need their sleep. They've got a lot to do tomorrow. Gotta find some gold!

CHAPTER 6

EARLIER THAT AFTERNOON, KORNAK AND Adria are walking to the dog shelter. They've been playing some rough football today, and their clothes are dirty. Adria is over her experience with her first dog. She wants to see the nicer ones.

Their conquest for gold turned out to be a few flimsy questions about the Super Bowl.

Oh well, on that one, not much info was gathered.

But this dog thing could still be in reach. It's just up the road. Kornak assures Adria that the dogs are there and could be bought. They have money (and dirt) in their pockets.

Adria still can't get over how beautiful the atmosphere is on this planet. She looks up at the blue sky with its white clouds meandering slowly by. She asks Kornak, "I wonder if there was ever a time when Nibiru had clean air like this?"

Kornak (acting like he is very knowledgeable) says to her, "They say there was, hundreds, maybe thousands, of years ago." He looks at her sincerely and says, "Maybe it was a blessing that we set down here. This planet is so beautiful."

Adria sounds excited saying, "And dogs! There are dogs here, Kornak! You did well—by accident, but good!" She picks up her pace as she talks. She walks ahead of him and turns around walking backward as she exclaims, "If we can get enough dogs to take to the new planet, then maybe we could repopulate there! Cats too, don't forget cats." As she's talking and walking backward, Kornak can see the place in the distance behind her. But he lets her keep talking a little longer. (She's so excited!)

Then he puts his hands on her shoulders and shushes her. Kornak tells her, "Hush a second, Adria. Listen!"

She looks surprised, saying, "What?" She's not sure why he shushed her.

"Listen!" he says, also very excited.

In the distance, the faint sounds of dogs barking can be heard. Like Kornak, Adria has never heard this sound before, so she doesn't know what it is. But she hears it though.

Holding her by the shoulders still, Kornak spins her slowly and points her toward the row of cages, and he says, "There they are!" She freezes, like she did with Lionel's dog. She puts her hands over her mouth and weeps lightly. She can see the dogs jumping in their cages, but they're still far away. She starts across the field (like she's a zombie or something), and Kornak slows her roll and explains, "We have to go through the front of the place, Adria." She snaps out of her trance as Kornak guides her back to the sidewalk they were on that leads to the red light.

But Adria's excitement is almost uncontainable. She keeps looking to the right at the bouncing figures in the cages. She is so anxious to get there that her pace gets faster. Kornak has to hurry his to keep up. Soon, they are at the light and hanging a right. Down two buildings and they are there, outside of the animal shelter! She can't believe it!

As they approach the door, two dirty-looking teenagers, Kornak gives Adria some instructions. Quietly, almost whispering, he tells her, "Now remember don't act so excited. Act like you've done this before. We don't want them to know who we really are. No big deal, okay?" Adria is nodding her head in agreement. They walk through the door, and inside is the same girl from yesterday.

"Good afternoon," she says enthusiastically. There haven't been very many customers in today, so she is happy to see them.

Kornak starts off saying, "We'd like to see some of your dogs." Adria nods her head yes, smiling, but not talking.

The girl responds, "Sure, come with me." She turns toward a door and opens it. "Is this your first time adopting?" she asks.

Kornak responds, "Yes, it is. We've lost a very dear pet recently."

The girl asks him, "Weren't you in yesterday, sir?"

"Yes, I was," he says.

"Your mom's dog died, right?" she asks.

"You do remember me," he says. "This is my sister," he says putting his arm around Adria.

"I'm sorry for your loss," the girl says to both of them. By now they are passing through a second door that leads outside to where the dog cages are! Adria is having trouble controlling her joy as they step into this area. Kornak tells the girl that they would like to buy his grieving mom several dogs. "That's fine, sir," she assures him. "Take as many as you like."

(She shouldn't have told them that!)

And there they are—dogs, of all shapes and sizes! Some have long fur and some short fur. But all are friendly and wanting to play. Adria can't believe her eyes and is still struggling to maintain her composure. *Just look at them all!* she thinks. Kornak is watching her closely, hoping she's not going to freak out and blow their cover. She is pretty pumped up though! As they stroll up to the row of cages, Adria wants to see the dog in the very first one. (This might take a while.) She squats down to get a better look and asks, "Can I see this one?" She sounds urgent.

"Why of course, ma'am," the girl says, hustling over with her keys. She lets the dog out, and it's a pretty, medium-size brown and white dog. It jumps right into Adria's waiting arms, tail wagging like crazy! Adria is in heaven holding this dog! She has been imagining this all her life, okay most of her life. She is crying slightly. The attendant girl notices and tries to help by describing the dog. She goes, "Her name is Molly. She's four years old . . . um . . . oh! She's good with kids. And she sure seems to like you!" Adria stands up straight and lets Molly stand up on her hind legs with her paws on Adria's belly. They are both loving this (especially Adria).

So Kornak has to step in a bit. He squats down petting Molly and says, "This one is very nice." He looks up at Adria and says gently, "Why don't we look at others?"

Adria agrees, again barely containing her enthusiasm and wiping tears off her cheeks, "Oh, yes," she says gleefully. "Let's look at others!"

The attendant girl is sort of overwhelmed by Adria's behavior. This is the biggest show of love she's ever seen. It's as though this girl (Adria) has never seen dogs before!

So the girl attendant (her name is Tanya) opens another cage for them. This dog is a big playful retriever mix. It has long fur and big ole face. Adria is loving it! But the phone rings in the office, and Tanya excuses herself cordially and goes to answer it.

So as Adria is frollicking with the big guy, Kornak kneels down with them. He wants to enjoy the moment too. He starts to notice though that as Adria is play wrestling with this friendly brute, she is changing. It takes Kornak a few moments to realize what he is seeing. Adria is shape-shifting into a dog! Her face has grown out like a dog's snout, and it has fur on it! Her neck becomes thick with fur. Kornak turns quickly to make sure the pound lady isn't around. Then he turns and semi-yells at Adria, "Stop it, Adria! You're shifting into a dog!" He then turns again to make sure Tanya is still busy on the phone. He's panicking slightly. So he jumps between the two, like a referee separates two boxers. Adria lets go of the dog and falls backward, on her butt. She definitely does have a dog look going. This would be hard to explain. Kornak helps her back to standing and urges her, "Give me some shape-shifting, girl! I need you back to human right now!"

Adria is kind of woozy and apologetic. "I'm so sorry," she says mumbling. "I didn't even know I was doing it." As she says this, she is changing back to her original reptilian look.

Kornak (with a bit of an angry tone) puts his hands on her shoulders again and says rather loudly, "No, no, no! Give me human! I need to see human!" So she regathers herself and concentrates on human form. Soon it comes to her. She has her human form back.

"That was a close one!" he says. Kornak is so relieved to see her getting her senses back.

And she's still apologizing about it. "I'm so sorry I did that. I almost blew it for us. I didn't even know I could do that. I didn't know it was happening!"

Kornak reassures her that all is okay and nothing bad came of it, luckily. He says with relief, "It's a good thing we were alone when that happened!"

After a few more moments, Tanya returns explaining that it was her boss on the phone. She says she told him she had to hurry him because she has customers. Kornak and Adria have regained their composure (just in time) and would like to look at more doggies. Tanya is happy to oblige. She puts the big rowdy dog back in his cage. Adria is already at the next cage asking excitedly, "Can I see this one?"

"You most certainly can," Tanya says smiling and already there with the key. Kornak is rolling his eyes but smiling too.

This next dog is a little bitty thing. She's a long-haired Chihuahua mix named Lucy. Tanya reaches down and picks her up and hands her to Adria, telling her that Lucy is a tame and well-behaved girl and also very affectionate. Lucy is bubbling with excitement!

Tail is just a waggin'. Adria holds her up near her face, saying softly to her, "Aren't you just the cutest little thing?" Lucy starts licking her face. Adria looks like she's in heaven again . . . uh-oh.

Kornak sees there may be another problem here, so he gently takes Lucy from her and suggests again they should check others out too. He gives Lucy back to Tanya, and Tanya puts her back in her cage. Tanya is trying to pretend that there's nothing weird going on here. But by now Adria is at the next cage wanting to see this one. It looks like a pitbull, very muscular and a big head. Adria and Kornak don't know that these dogs have a bad reputation. Some jerks raise them for fighting. But this one is so cool! He is dark brown with a little white on his chest, a beautiful example of his breed (he's on his very best behavior too because he wants out of this place). He's trying to wag his tail, but he doesn't have one, just a stump. But he's got that sucker going. Tanya gives a little background on him saying, "His name is Rusty, and he's four years old. He loves kids, but he is not good with cats, if you know what I mean." They don't. Adria squats down to greet him, rubbing his head and patting his sides. Kornak and Tanya stand by anxiously to see if she's gonna freak out on this one too. She doesn't. Adria seems to be calming down a bit. But she still wants to see the rest of these beautiful animals! She just can't believe this!

So Rusty goes back in his cage, and the group proceeds to look at more dogs. The next cage is a poodle. She looks kind of ruff (get it?). After that is another lab mix, very sweet dog.

Then there is one of those wiener dogs. It makes Adria laugh when she first sees it. Kornak has to shush her. He doesn't want Tanya to know that they've never seen anything like these animals before. But it seems like Tanya is picking up on this.

So to make a long story even longer, they look at every dog in the dang place. I'm serious.

Tanya is getting tired, but she is coming to like these two crazies. She sure hopes that they're going to buy something. And they don't disappoint her.

Kornak asks Tanya about their prices again. She perks up at that question. "They are thirty-five dollars each. Collars and leashes are five dollars each," she says, smiling. She leads them back inside (where the cash register is). As they get to the counter where they first met, Kornak and Adria start pulling cash out, in large sums from their front pockets, with dirt falling out too. Tanya chocks it up as another thing she's pretending isn't weird. Our heroes aren't sure how to count this stuff, so they are bumbling through it, hoping to get some help. Of course, Tanya sees them struggling, so she jumps in. They have hundreds and fifties, lots of 'em! Tanya can't believe how these two are handling this large amount of money, in their front pockets! She thinks to herself, *The guy doesn't have a wallet, and the girl has no purse or wallet of any kind. There are just tons of money in their pockets. And they can't count it. Could they be robbers? I'd think that robbers would be able to count, and they wouldn't be so open with such a large amount of money. And why would robbers go to the pound and buy dogs? This just gets weirder and weirder.* She stops thinking at that point and keeps counting.

She stacks the bills neatly on the counter, hundreds in one stack and fifties in the other.

Kornak and Adria look on as Tanya finishes stacking, telling them, "You've got a total of $1,700. I mean $1,750." She wants to keep it as simple as possible for these two. She then jokingly asks, "Did you guys want to buy some dogs today?"

Adria looks at Kornak smiling big and then back at Tanya saying, "Yes! Yes, we do!" Tanya thinks it is kind of odd that Adria doesn't look to Kornak for approval or agreement. She just takes charge! "How many can we get with this much currency?" Adria asks almost urgently.

Tanya has to whip out the calculator to do this one. She also wonders why Adria called it "currency." "Let's see," Tanya says. "How many times will 35 . . . I mean 45 . . . you do want collars and leashes, too, right?" Adria and Kornak both nod their heads yes. Tanya goes on, "So 45 into 1,750." Kornak and Adria look at each other. They're not sure what Tanya is talking about, but they trust that she knows what she's doing. Tanya suddenly realizes that she can't sell them all the dogs they want to buy. She can't sell them more than eleven. She explains that it's policy not to sell more than eleven, so as not to deplete their stock.

Our heroes look at her blankly. "Only eleven?" Kornak says, sounding disappointed.

Tanya tells him, "It's a rule. I'm sorry, sir."

Adria jumps in sounding excited, "Eleven it is then. Sell us eleven. Let's get on with it!" She is now leaning across the counter acting kind of hyper. "Can we go back and pick the ones we want?" she asks. Tanya agrees but tells them to put their money back away for now. And off they go, back to the dogs!

Soon, they come back to the front counter with their selections, all leashed up, eleven of them. They are of all shapes and sizes. Tanya rings them up, honestly of course. She wouldn't ever try to rip anyone off, especially two people who seem very naive about handling money, not to mention how unusual they were acting while looking at the dogs. She tells them that all the dogs have to be spayed or neutered but her vet is on vacation for two weeks, so they'll have to bring them back in at that time. Kornak and Adria agree not knowing what she's talking about. So she gets them squared away, gives them their change, and helps them and all their dogs toward the door. Kornak and Adria thank her sincerely for all her help. This has been a long afternoon for her. But she assures them they are very welcome. Also, Tanya wishes them good luck with all their new loved ones. They say goodbye to each other, and out the door go our heroes, toting eleven dogazoids.

Tanya has forgotten, in all the excitement, that she was supposed to get their information: name and address, phone number, and that stuff. She completely forgot. Lucky for the aliens, they don't have any of that! But Tanya forgot, so that's that for now. She still can't stop thinking how crazy the whole thing was. It's the weirdest sale she has ever made.

Kornak and Adria are outside now. It looks hilarious. They have never done this before.

The dogs are excited for being let out of those cages. They are all pumped up and getting tangled up with each other as they pull their new masters down the sidewalk. People have to move out of the way smiling as this mini stampede goes by. It's so funny, slightly out of control.

Once Kornak and Adria get their doggies to the main highway, they are getting better at it. The dogs are a little calmer now, and they all proceed down the sidewalk next to the road. They pass the neighborhood where they played football earlier in the day.

But just look at these cool dogs though! Adria can't get over it. Her dream has come true.

She has had this dream for so long, a love for animals she's never seen before except in pictures. Her persistence led to a search while stranded on a hostile planet!

And it paid off! What are the odds? And thank goodness for Kornak saving the day several times back there. She thinks, *We are taking dogs back to our ship! Although our voyage has had an emergency, we still hold hope to complete this mission and bring home these animals we all love so much. Our race hasn't seen dogs for several generations!* She's amazed that this happened. And she did it! Well Kornak found them; but she caused it to happen, by repeatedly asking Commander Zilog about it, knowing his main concern is finding gold and also knowing that he can be a grump. Luckily Zilog has a soft spot for dogs too. She pushed it just enough. And now they are returning to their ship with dogs from their exploration! Unbelievable!

Kornak's crowd of dogs is getting slightly ahead of Adria and her gang, as they get to the field where the ship is hiding. Adria has to pick up little Lucy because her tiny legs can't keep up with the bigger dogs. So she's carrying the little doggie. They're in the homestretch. It's dark out now, but that's okay, because they can see the trees. Kornak knows the way home.

They are both so wound up and elated about having dogs that neither has remembered to contact Zilog with the good news. So, as they are outside of the protective camouflage, Kornak stops or tries to stop to call him. "Green to blue, green to blue. Come in, blue," he says, speaking to his hand. His other hand is holding six leashes with rowdy dogs on the ends.

Zilog responds immediately. He's been anxious for someone to contact him. "This is blue. Come in, green," he says, sounding a little annoyed.

Kornak responds, very excited and out of breath, "Commander, we are returning from our mission." By now he and Adria and their dogs are in the synthetic forest and in view of the ship.

Zilog speaks to his hand still sounding mad. "Has your mission been successful?" he asks.

Kornak responds, "Partially but not completely, sir." Zilog asks, "How so, corporal?"

Kornak asks him, "Are you in the control center, sir?" "Yes, I am," Zilog says, sounding more impatient. "Look out the window, commander."

Zilog hurries over to the access port (or window) and looks out to see Kornak and Adria with eleven dogs, all tangled together and jumping about! Zilog's facial expression goes from semi-grouchy to extremely elated and overflowing with joy when he sees what his people have brought back! "Dogs!" he says out loud, very loud! "Dogs! Oh my!" He can't believe his eyes. He turns away from the window and heads out of the control center, moving quickly down the corridor toward the cargo bay.

He passes several passengers in the corridor who all think it is unusual to see him moving so fast. And he's got a glazed but happy look on his face. As he passes them, he looks their way saying loudly, pointing down the corridor as he runs by, "Dogs! They've got dogazoids!" He gets to the cargo area and sprints through it to the door control panel. And now the three passengers he just saw in the hall are catching up with him. Down goes the big door, and there they are—Kornak and Adria with eleven of their newfound friends! What a miracle!

Zilog and the three passengers are stunned by the sight of dogs! They all start down the ramp as though in shock to behold these beautiful creatures.

As they all embrace the dogs and play with them gleefully, Adria can feel that she has done a great thing. She walks over to Zilog and hands Lucy to him saying, "Try this one, sir. She's a loving little girl." Zilog takes her and holds her up near his face. Lucy is very happy to meet him, so she licks his cheek. He can't believe it yet. It happened too fast. Zilog didn't think he'd ever see any of these again. He holds her close, hugging her softly. She smells like Hiram (in a good way). Zilog remembers that smell of the one he loved so many years ago. Lucy is still trying to lick his face. It's making him giggle as he moves his face around to dodge her advances. It's so funny! He loves it!

All the others are having a grand time too! Now they have the dog leashes mostly untangled, and all the dogs are getting tons of love from everyone, barking and play-fighting and people-laughing. What a wonderful scene!

Kornak is loving all the joy the dogs have bestowed, as more people are coming down the ramp to see. He and Adria modestly step aside a bit so the others can enjoy. The two are also kind of tired from that crazy dog stampede coming back from the animal shelter (not to mention playing football earlier). They've had a physical day.

So anyway, meanwhile on the lonely country road that passes near where the ship is hidden, a car is coming. Uh-oh. This can't be good. The aliens are enjoying a nice little time with their dogazoids. But they have let their guard down somewhat. With the big ramp being down, light from inside the cargo bay is spilling outside, illuminating the area.

So the car approaches, and the two guys in it notice that there is something going on in those woods nearby, maybe a bonfire. These two guys, Tom and Jerry, can see shadowy figures moving around. They both stare as they drive by. You see, these guys are looking for a bonfire.

Earlier in the day, a friend was telling these two wild and crazy guys that a bunch of people were gonna have a bonfire out this way. Maybe they could pitch in and get a keg. That's why Tom and Jerry are driving on this road, looking for that keg party!

By now, they have driven by the light in the woods, but they're talking about it. Tom tells Jerry, "I think that might have been it."

Jerry says, "It sure didn't look much like a fire. It looked pink or something."

"Do you think we ought to go back and check it out?" Tom asks. "Sure," Jerry answers, "let's go see. It sure looked kind of weird though."

Tom pulls their car into someone's driveway, backs out, and shoots back the other way.

They want to find their friends and perhaps have a few beers with them. It's what young adults do in a hick town!

While that's going on, at the ship, Commander Zilog has herded everyone up the ramp and into the cargo area. He wants to get the dogs inside and safe. Then he closes the big door or ramp making it very dark outside. Inside, everyone is moving their jubilation up the corridor to the rec area.

Outside though, the total darkness has Tom and Jerry confused. (Their friends make fun of them for having those coincidental names.) But anyway, they don't see the lights any more.

Tom can't believe it. As he drives, he is pointing toward the woods saying, "Where did it all go? I know I saw lights in those woods! And it looked like people moving around!" He's now applying the brakes.

Jerry can't believe it either. He's also staring at the woods in disbelief. "It was just all lit up," he says softly. "What in the world?"

By now Tom has stopped the car in the grass next to the road, and they are both staring and mumbling about it. Tom is saying, "I know those woods were lit up. It wasn't even five minutes ago!"

Jerry is also amazed saying, "We just went by here. This is unbelievable." He looks at Tom with a frightened face and asks, "Do ya think we should take a closer look?"

Tom isn't sure about that. "You mean drive across this field?" He says loudly, "I don't think we should. It probably gets muddy out there. Do you wanna get stuck? Because I sure don't!"

Jerry gets loud too. He goes, "Don't you want to see what's going on out there? There's gotta be something in those woods. We just saw it! Pull on out there, ya big chicken!" Tom gives Jerry a mad look and cuts the steering wheel to the right and guns the gas, creating a nice fishtail as they head toward the strange little forest. Tom and Jerry want to find out what's going on in those woods over there.

Inside the ship, the evening is marvelous. They don't know that they had let their guard down earlier, so they're just partying, kids running around and dogs barking. The rec room is full of joy.

They don't have any gold to fuel their ship, but that's okay for now. They have dogs! Everyone is taking turns loving and playing with their newly found friends.

The captain and crew are happy to see all the passengers enjoying the evening.

The dogs are like a crazy miracle. No one on this flight has ever seen them before (except for Zilog). So all are delighted by their new friends.

Zilog finds Kornak and Adria sitting with some of the passengers in the cafeteria. They have one of the small dogs among them, playing and romping around. As Zilog approaches their table, he is smiling. He sees that all are having a good time, including that little dog!

But Zilog wants to talk to his two crewmembers. All at the table quiet down for him to speak.

He starts, "You two have brought such joy to us all by risking your lives to bring us these dogs." The girl holding the little dog hands her to Zilog. It's Lucy. He was holding her earlier. He knows how cute and cuddly she is. He begins to laugh as he holds her up by his face, saying, "She is so sweet!" Then he looks back to Kornak and Adria and continues, "I'd like to have more if you two think it would be possible."

Kornak and Adria look at each other and smile. Zilog continues, "Let me contact my other mission's personnel (M and O) in the morning to see where they are and how close they are to acquiring gold and returning. Perhaps you two can get in another group of dogs before they get back. I'm confident they are making progress and we'll be out of here soon. But this," he holds up Lucy and says, "this is just wonderful!" He exhales heavily and says, "I hope you can bring us more."

Adria and Kornak are humbled at hearing their commander's praise. They blush a little. Then Kornak snaps out of it and says very militarily, "We'd be honored to go out again, sir. I assure you that we can complete the mission again."

Adria adds in, "We can start first thing in the morning, sir!" She sounds very enthusiastic!

Zilog (also very excited) says to all, "Done then!" He hands Lucy to Adria and moves on through the crowd of people gathered. What a good night this is!

But all good things must come to an end. The gathering tapers down, and eventually everyone goes to bed, after making beds for the dogs. And all are learning about cleaning up (bathroom stuff, you know).

Outside, earlier this evening, Tom and Jerry are plowing through a field that seemed dry at first. They can see the patch of woods that they thought were lit up. It's right in front of them.

Tom swings his car (1964 Chevy Biscayne) around to the left, parallel to the woods, but he feels it bogging down. And sure enough, they get stuck! Tom is furious at their misfortune. "Dammit, Jerry! How did I let you talk me into this?!" As he rants, he puts the car in reverse and slams on the gas. He's mad as all get out! And reverse doesn't help at all. The car just gets stuck worse. "Dammit! Dammit! Dammit!" Tom says loudly while banging the steering wheel. "Why did we do this?" Jerry doesn't know what to say. This was his idea. He feels terrible. So he tries to console his angry buddy by staying sensible. He tells Tom to go ahead and cut the engine so they can open the trunk (they need the trunk key). Tom lets out a big sigh, looks at Jerry, and reaches for the ignition. He turns it off, and the engine stops running. Dead silence. Tom then pulls the key out and hands the key ring to Jerry, implying all this was his fault so he can get out and pop the trunk. "Start getting the stuff out."

You see they have stuff in the trunk that will help them get unstuck (hopefully). They've been through this before. This car gets stuck somewhat frequently, especially during the rainy season. They've got two shovels and some odd-shaped pieces of plywood (that they found in someone's garbage one other night when they got stuck). They have the bumper jack that came with the car and a scissor jack that Jerry borrowed from his dad. It's covered with dry mud.

So as Jerry clamors around in the trunk, getting all the stuff out, Tom slowly drags his butt out of the driver seat. He's dreading this. The last time it happened, it took hours of busting ass to get it unstuck. He puts his left foot out into the mud. It's tall grass with mud under it. *Great,* he thinks.

So out comes the right foot, and Tom makes himself get up out of the car. He feels the cold mud against his flip-flopped feet, as he heads to the back of the car. *What a bummer!* he thinks.

Both guys have forgotten what brought them out here—the light in the woods. Now it's the furthest thing in their minds. They've got this other stuff going on now.

Back inside the ship, no one knows what's going on outside. They are oblivious. Everyone is going to bed, including Zilog. He says goodnight to any of the passengers left in the rec area and heads for his quarters. Out of the cafeteria he goes, down a hallway to some metal stairs, like on ships. He trudges up the stairs looking tired, perhaps showing his age. Down a small corridor and he is at his room. He waves his hand (the one he communicates with) in front of the doorknob. A clicking sound is heard, and he pushes the door open.

He doesn't realize it, but Lucy the Chihuahua mix has followed him from the cafeteria. She pops in right behind him as he steps in. She runs over to his bed and jumps up on it. Zilog is very amused by all this. *She snuck up on me,* he thinks as he laughs. He walks to the bed and sits down as Lucy rolls over on her back for a belly rub. He is happy to oblige. One belly rub is coming up! When he stops, the little dog pumps her front paws in unison wanting more. It's so cute.

It reminds Zilog of pleasant times with Hiram, romping around on the bed. He still can't believe their good fortune—finding dogs on an accidental emergency landing! *What are the odds?* he thinks. Now if only they can successfully continue on to the new planet.

So Zilog and Lucy continue playing on the bed for a few more moments before someone else walks in the open door. It's another dog, a larger one. It appears to be an Irish setter, with long burgundy-colored fur. Zilog didn't remember seeing this one with the others. And he was startled by its arrival at first, but that soon wore off. A quick glance at the dog's belly shows it to be a female (no doinker). So Zilog talks to her smoothly. "Come here, girl," he says as he pats his leg. "Come here, girl," he says again.

Then to his astonishment, the dog speaks back! It says, "Commander Zilog, it's me, sir, Adria." Zilog's mouth falls open with amazement! Lucy barks a few times. She's startled too.

Adria (the dog) goes on, "Sir, I hope this isn't inappropriate. I didn't know I was capable of this until today. It almost happened at the dog pound."

Zilog is still kind of blown away, but he takes a humorous attitude and assures her it's okay.

He tells her, "I do need you back in time to maintain your duties." "Oh yes, sir," the dog says. "I'll be at full capacity, sir."

Adria then jumps on the bed and starts playing gently with Lucy. She talks to her as they frolic. "You sure are a cute little thing, aren't ya? Did you follow your new daddy home? You did good, honey." They romp around a little more with Zilog watching and enjoying their doggy antics.

But then suddenly Adria jumps up and says, "I'll leave you guys now. I know it's late." She jumps down to the floor and looks at Zilog and goes on, "Good night, commander." She looks at Lucy and says goodnight to her too. Then she trots out the door. She's going back to the cafeteria to see if anyone is still up. Zilog is still very surprised about what just happened. It was amusing! He shakes his head and smiles as he closes the door. He has decided to keep Lucy here tonight. She can sleep on the bed with him. They are becoming good friends.

Back to where Mezruh and Orsello are, it's morning. The sun is peeking over the horizon. Mezruh and Orsello are still asleep in the truck in the parking lot of McDonald's. When suddenly, without warning, Mezruh's hand starts buzzing, waking both of them abruptly.

Zilog says, "Blue to red, blue to red. Come in, red."

Mezruh answers sleepily, "Good morning, commander."

Zilog replies, "It's good to hear you. Are you men okay?"

"Yes of course, sir. We have traveled a long way on a major highway, and we have reached a heavily populated area" (Richmond).

"Have you fueled your vehicle?" Zilog asks.

Mezruh answers, "Yes, sir. As a matter of fact, we did! And we did it very well I might say. It was a learning experience, sir. Orsello went inside the store with the currency and paid. He did great, sir!" Orsello gives Mezruh the shoulder shrug like to say "Nothing to it."

Zilog continues, "I know I can count on you guys. Is there any word on gold yet?"

Mezruh says, "Um . . . not yet, sir. But today should be the day we come up with something."

Zilog tells him, "That sounds good, my comrade (he sounds very enthusiastic). Keep me posted on your progress."

Mezruh responds, "Yes, sir. Commander, orders received."

Zilog goes on (as he always does), "Be careful, you two. We need you back here."

After the conversation with Zilog, Mezruh and Orsello know to start moving with motivation.

Orsello suggests, "Do you want to go ahead and put that booster on?"

Mezruh likes it. "Yeah," he says. "Let's do that. Let me pull this thing somewhere where we don't have so many people around." He starts the truck and pulls out of the parking space and onto the road. They are up and moving now by golly!

Just a little ways down is a big store (Walmart), with a big, mostly empty, parking lot.

Perfect. They pull the truck in an empty part of said parking lot.

Both of 'em get out and start working methodically. They know what they're doing. They both have put quite a few of these boosters on different vehicles.

The booster itself is tubular shaped. It looks fairly simple, about five feet long, with a small blower motor at one end. Control cables are coming off the same end. It has to mount at the bottom of the truck, at the rear. The spare tire is in the way, so it has to come out. The booster has its own mounting devices that resemble heavy-duty clamps that attach to most any beam. The guys get it hanging fairly fast. The hardest part is getting that spare tire out of the way. What a bitch that was! It was mounted in there tight!

Now, the two control cables have to be routed to the driver area, the dashboard. It takes a little while to make that happen, but they have done it. Two little knobs are mounted at the bottom of the dashboard, under the radio. (They like that radio.)

"Good enough!" Orsello says loudly. "Let me put that extra tire in the back, and we are ready to go." The booster is in place. So the boys get in the truck and head on out of the parking lot. Onto the road they go. They're on the hunt now, looking for gold.

They could also use a good restroom too. But they don't know how it's done here.

The guys have learned how to fuel one of these Earth vehicles. They know how the humans eat (by drive thru). But where do they go to do their business? Hmm. Mezruh drives on as they discuss this problem.

Mezruh says, "You can't just get out and go on the ground! That's for sure."

Orsello answers, "Yeah, you don't see anyone doing that."

Mezruh sees what looks like another food establishment (Burger King). There are cars in the parking lot, people moving about, and a drive-thru line like at McDonald's. But you can smell this place. They both notice the smell of food cooking (that's Burger King with that flame-broiled thing going on). And oh man it smells good.

So they park the truck, and both get out. They know they have to go inside to seek the dooky room. It's got to be here somewhere! As they step inside, they see the place is busy. People are in line ordering food, sitting at tables eating, and moving about in general.

The aliens try to blend in as best they can. But they are very unfamiliar with this setup.

So they sort of get in line to order, looking up at the readerboard that you order from. Orsello likes what he sees, colorful pictures of hamburgers and other stuff. It all looks so good, just like at the place last night (McDonald's) except now they're inside the food port. Mezruh thinks to himself, *This sure is better than eating that manna crap.*

So they decide to order some food as they scope the place out for the restroom.

Mezruh steps up to order for them. He tries what he has memorized from last night. He goes, "Can I have two number 3s with a Pepsi and a Diet Coke?" The kid types it all into the computer. Mezruh perks up to order more, "Oh and can you put a couple of Quarter Pounders in with that?"

The kid says, "Would you like Whoppers, sir? We don't have Quarter Pounders. This is Burger King." The kid rolls his eyes a little while Mezruh looks embarrassed.

He then says to the kid, "Whoppers you say. Well then make it Whoppers!"

During this time, Orsello has seated himself at a table around the corner from the ordering area. He has noticed people walking by, but not carrying food. *Hmm, that must be it back there!* he thinks.

But here comes his buddy with a tray full of delicious-looking food. Mezruh puts the tray on the table and picks up the empty cups. He holds the two stacked cups and says, "What am I supposed to do with these?" Orsello nods his head toward the drink fountain area. He has seen a few people using it, filling their cups with ice and soda. Mezruh sees it and says, "Oh well, what do you know?" He turns and heads for it.

Orsello says, "Get mine too. I'll watch the food." He starts picking through the goodies Mezruh brought. It's not the same as last night, but it all looks really good. When Mezruh returns with the drinks, Orsello is already pigging out.

Mezruh sees this and says to his buddy, "Slow down, spaceman!"

Orsello responds with, "This planet is great! The food here is—"

"Ssshhh," Mezruh says as he sits down. "Don't let anyone hear that. You'll give us away."

So they gobble up all the food without using what we call manners. They don't have any.

But they do okay by watching others around them. After just a few minutes, all their food is gone. Boom! There's a big mess on the table. Orsello sits back and sucks the last of his drink through a straw, making that gurgling sound. He lets out a big burp and says, "I'm going to the restroom."

Mezruh perks up and asks, "Do you know where it is?"

Orsello points with his thumb and says, "It's right back there." Mezruh looks back to where Orsello is pointing, and sure enough there are two doors.

So the guys both slide out of the booth and head for what looks to be bathrooms. They disregard the little signs that say "Men and Women." Mezruh goes into the men's room and Orsello the women's room. He encounters a lady in the ladies' room and says hello. The woman looks furious, doesn't say anything, and stomps out mad. Orsello wonders what that was about, and then he looks around until he sees the stalls with toilets. *This must be it,* he thinks. And he proceeds to do his business. He sees that there's a door that closes. *Huh,* he thinks, *wonder what this is for.*

Mezruh is doing okay in the men's room. There is a guy in there washing his hands and then using the blow-dryer. Mezruh walks on by, but he studies the guy as he does. It is just his nature to watch others and learn from them. He finds the stalls with toilets okay, and he too does his business.

So they blow up both bathrooms at the same time, stinking out the whole dining room. People are leaving in a hurry. It stinks so bad.

It seems that alien poop is much stinkier than human poop. As they come out of the bathroom at about the same time, the dining area that was full of people and hustle-bustle is now empty.

Several employees are standing at the far end, near the ordering area. It's like they are peeking around the corner at our heroes.

As the boys head out the door, the employees' peeking looks turn to angry stares. People are standing outside in the parking lot holding their food. They too are staring angrily and mumbling jabs at the guys as they walk by, things like "You guys stink like hell" and "What did you guys eat? You sure ruined my breakfast!" "Jerks!" someone yells. "You guys suck!"

The boys just ignore them and head to their truck. As they are getting in, Orsello wants to know what the big deal is, saying, "I guess these people's poop doesn't smell."

So off they go, leaving the angry crowd behind. But as they pull out, something miraculous catches Mezruh's eye. Right next to Burger King, they didn't even see it when they pulled in, is a gold store—a big gold store! It looks like it used to be something else, maybe a department store. But now it's a big gold store! There's a guy out front dressed like a cowboy, waving a sign that says, "We buy gold." Our boys can't believe their good fortune! Mezruh pulls the truck right on in there! Both are excited!

CHAPTER 7

Earlier that morning onboard the ship, Zilog has just contacted his "boys in the field," Mezruh and Orsello. They have assured him that good results are coming. Zilog has confidence in them.

He knows they'll do whatever it takes to obtain the gold they need to get them off this planet. Even if they might need to get a little rough, it's got to be done. Hopefully no one gets hurt.

Zilog then changes gears in his mind. He summons Kornak and Adria to the control room.

They arrive very shortly. Both are excited about having their commander's praise and of course about going out again, for dogs!

Zilog speaks first, "Good morning, comrades!" He is smiling. "I have just spoken with our men in the field, and they assure me that sometime today they will be back. I'm not sure when though."

Kornak asks, "Shall we run our mission, sir?"

"Yes," Zilog answers, "but the time to go is now though. We don't know when the gold mission will return."

Adria looks excited and says, "Orders received, sir!" She is anxious to go!

Zilog says very enthusiastically, "Go then, you two!" He waves his arm and smiles. "Be safe," he adds.

Zilog is growing fonder of his nephew, now that Kornak is helping the situation in such an unusual way, a joyous way! How could Zilog stay mad? This is a great thing they are doing, if successful. Bringing dogaziods to the new planet? Everyone there would be amazed! They will say, "Where in heaven's name did you guys get these?!" Unbelievable!

So anyway, Kornak and Adria are off on their way walking. Both have morphed into teenagers again as their commander instructed. They both know they have to be urgent on this mission. They are walking faster than usual. But they talk pleasantly as they walk, telling about their past and such. They are becoming closer friends. Adria has long forgiven Kornak for his mistake, especially since he brought her to dogs! She can't believe the good fortune that has been bestowed upon them—the miracle of dogs.

They pass where they played football and Disc War yesterday (crazy Earth games). There's no time for any of that today though. It was fun, and they made some friends, but now their mission is urgent. There's no time for socializing. No one knows when the gold will be arriving, but they look to take off soon thereafter.

On board the ship, Zilog has Lucy, and he is holding her against his chest. He is petting her and talking to her softly. It feels so good for him to have a dog again. He's in the cargo bay, and the ramp is down, showing a beautiful day outside. Passengers are outside with all the other dogs, frolicking and laughing—a very tranquil scene.

As per their commander's orders, all are staying in human form. It is so very important that they look the same as the beings here. Zilog figures like "Where do you hide, a tree? In the forest of course!" Zilog is very concerned that if they stayed in their original state, which is lizard-like in appearance, the Earth race might attack and destroy them—only because of their appearance. (I know. I said that already.)

So, earthlike it is, just a bunch of humans playing with their dogs (next to a giant spaceship).

Hopefully of course they won't be discovered, and no defenses will be necessary.

Then suddenly, Zilog's hand buzzes. It's the boys—ahem—his comrades in the field.

It's Mezruh calling, "Red to blue, red to blue. Come in, blue."

Zilog answers, "This is blue. Talk to me, Mezruh!" He sounds cheerful, hoping to hear good news.

Mezruh goes on. He sounds excited too. "Sir, we're in sight of a very large gold operation. It looks like there is more than enough gold here to power us all the way to the new planet. We're going to go inside and check the place out and then make our move."

Zilog becomes wary. "It worries me, Mezruh. I don't want to lose either of you guys. Don't get too crazy in there. Okay?"

Mezruh answers, "Yes, sir, we've got this."

Zilog, still sounding worried, says, "Okay then, keep me informed."

"Yes, sir! Orders received."

Zilog resumes petting Lucy with his communication hand. He's worried now though. His mood isn't as light as it was a few moments ago. He doesn't want any harm to come to his guys, but the gold is so needed.

He goes back into the ship and into the command center, where he sits in his chair, still holding Lucy. Petting a dog helps to soothe a worried mind.

Meanwhile, Mezruh and Orsello are getting pumped up for the next stage of their mission. They are parked in the parking lot of this "gold store" as they call it. It's a big place.

Mezruh speaks, "So we go in, look around some, and find where the big pieces of gold are."

Orsello replies, "Then when we're ready, boom! I morph and you don't. You have to drive this thing when we're ready to leave."

"Are you sure you're okay with that? Your clothes are going to get ruined. You know that, right?" Mezruh asks.

"Sure, homey, I can get real big and ugly! The clothes flying off adds to the effect." Orsello tells him.

Mezruh adds, "And scary, don't forget scary!"

"Got it! Rowrrr!" Orsello holds his hands up in scare mode. "Rowrr!" he says again.

"Yeah, that's it! That's good." Mezruh looks amused.

Orsello responds, "Now you've got to be grabbing gold too. Once I get everybody moving, I'm probably gonna bust open some of those glass counters, and you jump in and get the biggest pieces."

Mezruh acknowledges, "Got it. We're gonna do this!" He giggles.

"Let's go!" Orsello says looking pumped!

So they get out of the truck and head for the door. But they've parked pretty far away.

Orsello stops and taps Mezruh on the shoulder to stop too. Mezruh says, "What?"

Orsello suggests, "Maybe you should bring the truck up closer to the door, for our exit."

"Good idea. I'm on it." He turns and heads back to the truck, while Orsello keeps walking toward the store. He gets to the door, and he stands and waits patiently, just a peaceful-looking old guy waiting for his old guy friend. The cowboy dances by with his sign. Mezruh pulls the truck up in the fire lane in front of the door. Then he pulls down a little ways so as not to block their hasty exit. He parks it right there, shuts it off, and gets out. He joins Orsello at the door, and they go in together. This is it!

The place is beautiful inside—display counters (glass), nice carpet, soft music playing, and a lot of greenery. Hanging plants are all around. The place is kind of swanky.

People are milling about shopping for jewelry. No one speaks loud.

Not sure why, that's just how gold stores are. Shhh!

The security guy is hanging around one of the back counters. He's talking with two employees of the store. He has a gun. You can see it there on his hip as he slouches across the counter. His day is going fine so far. But that's about to change!

Our boys are just meandering about, checking out the large variety of gold products available to the consumer. Har-har. On the right as they walk is a large display of gold teapots and cups with saucers. Mezruh glances at it as he passes. They stroll on toward the back. As they come near the cluster of people that include the security guy, Orsello stops and pretends to be looking at jewelry. Mezruh pulls up beside him and mumbles, "Is it time?"

Orsello mumbles back, "Are you ready, partner?" Mezruh says, "I'm ready. Let's do this."

Orsello's appearance begins to change rapidly. He becomes larger. His head becomes lizard-like with a big snout full of teeth. His clothes rip as his body expands and his hands turn into claws. He is now a huge monsterlike being, and he lets out a terrible shriek! It's sort of like a cross between an elephant and a grizzly bear—crazy- sounding shriek! He whirls to face the people nearby him, who are already frozen with fear. Then he starts walking toward them!

But they are so frozen with fear that they don't move at all! They just stand there in shock.

Orsello the monster then turns away from this group of thoroughly terrified people and roars out into the store. People are so surprised at this display of craziness that it takes a few moments for anyone to respond.

A giant shrieking dinosaur-looking thing? And it looks pissed off too. No one has ever seen anything like this! Then the monster starts breaking glass displays, banging on them with the palms of his big ole lizard hands, making a huge mess. Glass goes flying around everywhere. And he's screeching at the same time!

Now all the gold customers are gathered at the far end of the store. They are terrified of this hideous creature that seemed to come out of nowhere!

Mezruh is gathering gold. He's going for the bigger pieces too! Orsello stops screeching and smashing for a second and says to Mezruh in his regular voice, "How am I doing?"

Mezruh whispers, "You're doing great, buddy!" His arms and pockets full of gold, he tells Orsello, "I've got about all I can carry. I'll be heading for the truck. Grab some more, and let's get out of here!"

Orsello says "Okay" followed by another loud screech. Then he turns back toward the people at the back of the store, who are starting to move around a bit. The security guy pulls his gun as Orsello approaches him. The monster is looking just to horrify, showing big teeth and that terrible screeching! The poor security guy trembles with fear, and the gun just falls to the floor. The other two people he had been chatting with are crumpled on the floor behind the counter. They won't be putting up a fight either, which is good because Orsello doesn't want to hurt anyone. He just wants to scare and then gather gold, which he does! He screeches at the guard and the people on the floor one last time and then turns toward one of the glass counters that he had previously broke.

The big pissed-off lizard-looking monster is now grabbing gold items from their display cases and holding them against his body. He then runs to another display and does the same. Now his arms are full of gold items and other junk. Can you imagine how crazy this must look to the people still trapped inside?

But then suddenly, without warning, the store alarm goes off, blaring louder than sin!

Orsello thinks, *Time to go!*

Outside, a few minutes earlier, Mezruh had just made it to the truck and got in with his armloads of loot. Then he notices a cop has pulled up behind him. Mezruh is watching the police in his mirror, but he is unsure who these guys are. The cops are running his tag number, and sure enough it comes back as stolen from several counties away.

So Mezruh is just sitting there acting natural. He's hoping his buddy will hurry up with his shopping (har-har). The cops start getting out of their car. They've got a job to do. See what this guy's story is. Then, as they head toward the Chevy truck, all hell breaks loose! First, the store's alarm goes off loud as hell. This causes them to flinch really bad, and both reach for their guns.

Then a few moments later, the whole front window of the place comes crashing out, as a large lizard-looking monstrosity (covered with stolen gold) barrels through it. Glass goes flying everywhere (again).

The two cops are frozen with terror as the "thing" does a roll on the sidewalk. He gets up and does his screech which is even louder than the store alarm going off! Both of the cops stagger backward in total disbelief.

Then the monster stands up and shows his height to be about eight or nine feet tall. This causes the policemen to retreat to their car doors. The monster then bends down to pick up the gold he dropped. The poor cops can't believe what they're seeing, a giant lizard man stealing gold and not being very sneaky about it either! The cowboy is holding his sign in front his body like a shield.

So Orsello jumps into the back of the truck with all the gold he can carry, and Mezruh takes off, leaving people, including the police, staring in disbelief. They gradually start coming out of it, and the cops jump in their car to give chase.

Our heroes are feeling pretty good about themselves. They are pulling out of the parking lot onto the road that leads to the big road (the interstate). Mezruh knows to stay near the big road.

It's the one that takes them back to the ship.

As they are pulling out of the parking lot onto the road, "monster boy" Orsello pulls himself up to the back window of the truck. It's got one of those little slide windows in the middle. Orsello still can't get his big lizard head in to talk to his buddy. So he pulls the glass out on the passenger side and the sliding window. That's better. He then sticks his head in to talk to Mezruh.

Orsello says cheerfully, "How we doing up here, bro?" He looks down and sees all the gold Mezruh gathered lying on the seat and floor, mixed with McDonald's junk.

Mezruh barks back excitedly, "I'm doing just fine! And you sure did a good job back there!" He stomps on the gas as he talks. "You were a scary act! You had everyone going backward!"

"I know! It went well I must say!" Orsello answers. Just then a green light turns yellow, and Mezruh has to slam on the brakes. This is the same light where McDonald's is where they ate yesterday. How nice. Outside McDonald's is another police car and the girl from yesterday who thought our heroes seemed suspicious. She's telling the police all about it too.

As she speaks to them, she looks up when she hears brakes screeching. It's Mezruh, now sitting kind of sideways at the light. The girl freaks. She stands up straight, points at Mezruh's truck, and says, "That's the guy and the truck right there!" She is not sure what she is seeing in the back of the truck, maybe a parade float or something. But she starts yelling to the cop, "That's him. That's the guy with the fifty-dollar bills!"

And besides all that, here comes the other cop with his lights on and siren blaring. So the cop at McDonald's sees this, and he takes off too. But someone backing out of a parking space in Mickey D's doesn't see the police car barreling by and causes a crash in the parking lot.

Then Mezruh's light turns green, and he takes off! He doesn't care what's going on at McDonald's. (He doesn't know it involves him.) So he guns it, and that other cop is real close since Mezruh stopped at the light. The policeman at the wheel wonders out loud, "Why in the world would someone who just made a huge scene at a jewelry heist stop at a red light with us in hot pursuit?"

The other cop agrees saying, "Beats the crap out of me! He did it though! And we still don't know what that is in the back there."

"He sure likes his bling!" the other cop says, as they follow close behind them, lights flashing red and blue. Siren blaring loud as can be!

Mezruh knows which way to get them back to the ship. He hangs a right at the next light, and up on the interstate they go. Cops are right behind them. Mezruh says to his buddy, "I think these guys are after us. See if you can get 'em off our tail!"

"Check!" Orsello responds. He pulls his big head out of the window and stands up in the back of the truck. He then becomes unstable and sits back down. He crawls to the tailgate and hangs out as far as he can.

The poor cops are wondering what this thing is going to do next. It looks like it's about to jump out of the truck at them. It just might!

Orsello does his loud screech thing, but he can't scream louder than the cop's siren. But it does scare the cops though. They still don't know what to make of this thing. The cop driving, an older kind of senior cop, says, "Take a couple of shot at it! No, wait. Maybe we shouldn't!"

His younger partner is angry and excited, yelling, "They robbed a jewelry store! But what is that thing?"

Senior cop responds, "I don't know. I just don't know!"

You have to give these brave policemen tons of credit for chasing this wild-looking monster. They had to overcome the shock of the early part of this episode, and they did. And here they are in hot pursuit! Go, boys! Men in blue never give up!

At this point, Orsello decides to start throwing stuff. Keeping in mind he's not to kill anyone, he picks up the spare tire (rim and all) with one hand. He holds it up high over his head, and he looks at the cops as if to say, "You want me to throw this?" He shakes it threateningly as if saying, "I'll do it!"

The officers can't believe the strength of this thing! He's holding a spare tire over his head, shaking it like it's a teddy bear or something. It's got to weigh eighty or ninety pounds. That lizard thing must be strong! Show some respect, guys!

Mezruh calls back to Orsello, "How you doin' back there? Are they still with us?"

Orsello, putting the spare down, answers (he has to yell over the police siren), "They're still back here alright. I think they want to ask us some questions!" He then turns and roars at them again causing both cops to jump, and their car swerves to the left. This monster is still pretty scary!

So the younger cop decides he has had enough from this giant lizard, gold-thieving son of a—anyway, he decides to bring the shotgun out. The other cop approves. He's had enough of this thing too. He tells his young partner, "Shoot it, Johnny, before it has another chance to throw stuff at us! Don't take no more crap off of this thing! It is dangerous! Shoot it!"

The senior cop now has his head together enough to call this crazy situation in to dispatch. He speaks frantically into his microphone, "Um central dispatch? This is car 91. Uh we got something crazy going on . . . southbound on I-95." He stops and takes a deep breath and tries to gather himself further. At the same time, the other officer is positioning himself to take a shot.

He's hanging out the passenger side window, waving that shotgun!

Orsello, still in monster form of course, sees this guy about to take a shot at them. He leans down to the window he tore out a few minutes ago and puts his head inside to ask a question.

"Hey, bro, can we get that booster going?" he asks.

Mezruh has already been messing with the little control knobs to get it going. He recognized that the situation was going bad, so he was already messing with it.

Orsello sees the police officer raising his gun to shoot, so he picks the spare back up. He holds it about chest height with both hands. And he throws it, about like you throw a medicine ball! The spare hits the cop car in the right front headlight area and bounces back, almost killing the poor guy as he falls back into the car. He loses the shotgun, but it falls inside the car to the back seat.

Orsello sticks his head back into the truck and says to Mezruh, "It's getting crazy back here. How's that booster coming along?"

Mezruh, now leaning down where the little knobs are, says back (not very calmly), "I'm working on it! I think I've almost got it. It's just not lighting!"

By now the cop has his gun back, and he's hanging out the window again. He's mad now after that tire almost hit him! Sheesh! He's all fired up! And he's ready to shoot!

Meanwhile, the older policeman is chattering into the mike, trying to explain what's happening out here. He says, "It's a brown Chevy truck." (BOOM!) His partner gets a shot off. Miss!

The senior cop goes on explaining, "They robbed the gold outlet store on seventy-third street. But get this." He starts to go on, "This thing in the back—" (BOOM!) Another miss! He starts back trying to talk, "It's a great big—WHOA! Look out!" The monster threw a big box of tools that was in the truck. It's a perfect hit. Nobody gets hurt, but tools fly everywhere, and the windshield of the cop car is wasted. But these cops aren't giving up. They're tough as nails! The senior cop is now hanging out his window so he can see to drive and keep up with this craziness. He's not talking on the radio anymore. It's lying in broken glass on the seat.

The other officer is regrouping, putting shells in the gun. The toolbox is wedged in the windshield, dashboard area of the police car. So now the shotgun man can just lay the gun on the toolbox to steady it. Great! (That was sarcasm.)

Orsello sees the cop lining up his next shot. So he grabs the four-way lug wrench and slings it like it's a ninja star. He throws it hard too! So the four-way wrench whizzes into the cops' car near the shotgun rider's head. This causes him to dive sideways into the other cop (the driver) causing him to briefly lose control of the car.

It is at this point that Mezruh finally gets the power booster lit off. It makes a muffled boom sound, and Orsello knows that sound well. The big scary monster is now doing a victory dance in the back of the truck, on his knees, pumping his arms in the air! He knows that booster is gonna save them. It lets out a cloud of black smoke like a big burp. The smoke goes right into the police car, clouding their judgment for a few seconds. When the smoke clears, the cop with the shotgun starts looking to take another shot, but our boys in the Chevy truck are way ahead of them now.

The booster is doing its job. As Mezruh slowly pushes the acceleration control, their speed increases dramatically.

Orsello has stopped his victory dance and is now sitting comfortably in the corner of the bed behind the window he broke out, one elbow on the back window and one elbow on the wall of the bed. He looks like he's relaxing poolside at some high-end hotel, waving at slower cars as they fly by them. The cops can't believe it. They were right on these guys' butts just a few seconds ago. And now they're about a quarter mile behind and losing more distance fast.

The truck has an orange flame coming out of the back of it that wasn't there before. Crazy!

Mezruh sees a good stretch of open lane ahead of him. So he decides to open up that booster some more! Also, at this point, he starts using the other lever too, the one that controls altitude and steering. Orsello sees him starting to use the second knob, and he gets excited, because he knows what's about to happen. He braces himself where he is sitting.

So with the speed about 200 mph or so, Mezruh works the lever that brings it up off the ground, similar to a plane or jet and also, strangely though, similar to the Nazi V-1 missile in World War II. Rumor has it that the Nazis had extraterrestrial help with their secret "mega" weapons. They were so far ahead of the allies in this area. They had to have had help.

But anyway, back here in our story, Mezruh moves the lever that takes them off the ground, and it does just that! The Chevy truck with the flame coming out the back is now flying.

People in their cars are amazed! A truck goes roaring by startlingly loud, just over them, flying! The cops of course are seeing this from a ways back, but it still looks so unbelievable.

It's a truck taking off like a jet, going incredibly fast. After just a few seconds, it's a tiny dot in the sky. The cops watch as it disappears. They look at each other as if to say, "You saw that too, right?" The older cop pulls the car off the road at this point. Why keep going? The windshield is smashed out with a big toolbox wedged in it. Besides, the chase is over. It's over! Whatever that thing was is gone. They still can't believe it. It happened so fast. The senior cop turns off the siren but leaves the lights flashing. They are both in shock, but still functioning. They are covered with broken glass, as is the seat. The younger officer puts the shotgun down, nothing to shoot at. It all happened so fast.

CHAPTER 8

A SMALL CESSNA AIRPLANE IS flying peacefully along on this nice sunny afternoon. It is flown by a couple, husband and wife. Tom, the husband, is the pilot. He's taking his wife, Charlene, to a new doctor in a city far away. Charlene is having psychological difficulties. She tries to keep it under control, but she swears she sees things that just aren't there. But it's okay for her to be open and talk about it. So she and Tom talk openly about her problem and solution as they fly.

Tom speaks, "This new doctor is going to help, hon. I just know it. He's the best in his field." Tom pats her on the leg assuredly. He knows she's very worried about this.

"I sure do see some weird stuff," she says. "I hope this guy can help, but isn't this a nice day to be in the sky?" She's trying to change the subject.

"Beautiful!" Tom answers with enthusiasm. "Nary a cloud in the sky!" he says looking around.

They both take sips from their coffee. They had stopped at Starbucks on their way to the airfield.

When suddenly, on their right, a Chevy truck appears in the sky and goes zooming by.

Tom and Charlene are taken by surprise! Still holding their coffees, they watch amazed as it passes. And in the back is some unidentified creature, wearing a lot of gold. He's leaning back, looking comfortable. He smiles and waves as they pass. The couple can't believe what they are seeing! Tom exclaims loudly, "Trucks don't fly! And that big lizard thing—what the devil is that?!" His is voice getting very high at the end.

Charlene has no response. She's just staring straight ahead. Finally she mumbles softly, "You saw that, right?"

So the flying Chevy moves to the horizon quickly and disappears. On board the truck, Mezruh is giggling about scaring those people. He thought that was pretty funny! Orsello thought so too, giving them that little wave. They both laugh a little, relaxing some. Danger is no longer near. Those cops back there gave them hell though!

Mezruh reaches for the radio knobs and turns it up. It's playing a really good REO Speedwagon song called "Back on the Road Again." It's a killer jam, a lot of fast guitar. The boys love it!

Orsello pokes his big head into the cab and asks, "Any more of those burgers left?" He rustles the bags on the seat and yes! He finds one! It's a cold quarter pounder. He puts the whole thing (box and all) in his mouth and then spits the box out. Mezruh watches with disgust.

Mezruh then turns his head out the window looking down. He has to make sure he stays parallel to the big road (I-95) that will lead them back to the ship. Also, he has throttled the booster down like airline pilots do when their plane reaches desired altitude.

Mezruh then spots two flying machines (helicopters) off in the distance. He has to stay his course. Hopefully these guys won't bother our heroes.

And we should now leave all this on hold for a few moments, so we can catch up with the other heroes in the story. It gets pretty crazy too!

At the dog pound earlier that day, the mood is uneasy. The girl (Tanya) who sold Kornak and Adria eleven dogs yesterday is telling her boss about how strange the deal was and how the girl (Adria) acted like she had never seen dogs before.

Tanya tells her boss (Mr. Jenkins) that the whole thing seemed surreal. "She (meaning Adria) broke down and cried when she saw the first one and then stayed crying for a good while before she calmed down." Mr. Jenkins listens intently as Tanya goes on, "And another thing that was strange was how they paid!"

Jenkins inquires, "How was it strange, Tanya?"

"Well," she goes on, "the young man and the young woman both had wads of fifty- and one hundred-dollar bills that they carried in their pants pockets—no wallets, no purse, none of that." She adds, "They couldn't count very well either. I had to help them. And the money seemed dirty, kind of gritty" (from football of course).

Mr. Jenkins is astonished by all this. He's never had anything like this happen before. So he has a decision to make. Should he bring the police into this matter? After all, an armored car had been stolen two days prior. And nobody has been caught yet either.

So Mr. Jenkins does the right thing and calls the sheriff officers out. He wants to make sure that his employee doesn't get in any trouble for taking part in this deal.

When the police arrive, Mr. Jenkins and Tanya both begin describing what happened and how out of place it all seemed. The cops are polite, writing stuff down and gathering as much information as possible. They agree that the transaction seems to be suspicious if not downright illegal. And those two were probably the ones who stole the armored car.

As the four people (two policemen and two dog pound employees) are discussing the case, Kornak and Adria pop in the door. They saw the sheriff's car outside but didn't think anything of it, just a brightly painted green and white car.

Tanya freaks out when they walk in. Her eyes get big! She nudges Mr. Jenkins with her elbow and whispers urgently, "That's them! That's them!"

The cops look up from their writings and turn to see who these bad guys are. It's a couple of teenagers who don't look capable of jacking an armored truck.

Kornak and Adria say hello cheerfully. They remember Tanya from yesterday, and they assume everything is okay. Everything is not okay!

Officer Brooks picks up on Tanya's whispering and becomes very attentive toward these two kids. He nudges his partner Sapp and says out loud, "These are the two people who were in here yesterday?"

Tanya responds nervously, "Yes, officer, this is them."

Officer Brooks starts in with some questions. "Were you two in here yesterday?" he asks.

Kornak and Adria respond with "yes."

Brooks goes on, "It's been reported that you two bought quite a few dogs."

Kornak answers calmly, "Yes, sir, we did." (He's not being cocky or arrogant.)

Officer Brooks then asks, "And did you pay for the animals using fifty-and one hundred-dollar bills?"

Kornak answers, "I believe so, yes."

"Well, son, two days ago an armored truck was stolen downtown, and the currency involved in this incident was mostly fifties and hundreds." The officer goes on, "Now, can you explain where you two (he looks sternly at Adria) came up with a vast amount of fifty- and one hundred-dollar bills yesterday?"

All the others are watching the interview as though it is a movie or Perry Mason or something. It's Kornak's turn to talk now. He comes up with a doozy of a story that is adapted from his own past. Hopefully he can make it fit here. "Well," he starts, "my uncle is a gambler, and he carries a lot of cash on him. He hates banks. And so he hit big the other night, and it just so happened on that same night, my mom's dog died."

Tanya pipes up and says, "I remember him telling me about his mom's dog dying." She acts like she's trying to help now, even though she's the one who brought all this up.

Kornak goes on, "Yeah, my uncle gave me a bunch of money, mostly fifties. Then he told us to go and buy as many dogs as we could, to soothe her."

Officer Brooks seems like he's not buying this story at all. It sounds very shaky. He says, "Well we're going to run the serial numbers on the bills you used to see if they are stolen. But in the meantime, I'll need to see some ID from both of you. Driver's license, ID card, what do you have?" Kornak and Adria look at each other.

Adria tells the policeman, "We don't drive, sir, so we don't have anything for ID."

Officer Brooks is starting to look impatient. "Well then give me your names," he says as he pulls his notebook and pen up near his face and readies himself to write.

Kornak goes first, "My name is Mike."

Officer Brooks writes down Mike and says, "Mike what?"

Kornak didn't know he had to come up with a last name. He looks around the room. He sees a poster that warns of heartworms in dogs. "Heart!" he says. "Mike Heart."

Brooks says loudly, "Heart? Spell it."

Kornak glances at the poster again nonchalantly and spells it for this not very nice cop, "H, E, A, R, T."

Officer Brooks looks skeptical, but he writes it down. He then looks at Adria. It's her turn. "And you, miss. What's your name?"

Here goes Adria with her crazy fake name. "Totzke," she says proudly. Kornak looks the other way and rolls his eyes.

Impatient Officer Brooks says, "Spell it!"

Adria says, "T-O-T-Z-K-E. Totzke."

Brooks says, "I've never heard that name before." His stern suspectful attitude turns soft for a minute. He goes on, "And what is your last name, ma'am?"

"The same as his, Heart. I'm his sister."

Kornak looks surprised that she would call herself his sister. He feels honored in some weird way. He thinks to himself, *She did that so smoothly, very believable.*

Officer Brooks asks, "So it's Mike and Totzke Heart?"

Kornak and Adria both agree, "Yup. That's our names, all right."

Brooks continues the interrogation, "And where do you two reside?" He asks next, "What's your address?" Once again Kornak Adria look at each other. Neither has an answer to that one.

Kornak speaks up, "Um well, we're new here. We just moved in. I haven't memorized our address yet." He hopes the cops will buy it, but they don't.

Officer Brooks regrets to tell them that they'll have to accompany them to the police station, to answer some more questions and wait while those bills are analyzed. The officer then puts his little notebook in his shirt pocket and gently takes Kornak by the back of his arm and starts to point him toward the door.

Kornak pulls away from him and says loudly, "We don't have time!" He is thinking about the ship being ready for takeoff any time now. So he backs away from the officer, determined to not be taken into custody! "We're not going with you!" Kornak proclaims sternly. Officer Brooks's face turns angry. He was hoping these two youngsters weren't going to resist him and Sapp in any way. But they did, especially Kornak. He can't help it. Not only has he been angered, but he also fears being captured. So he has to do it. He sees both cops reaching for their tasers. He doesn't know what those things are, but it can't be good. He looks to Adria as if to say, "Here goes!"

With the officers approaching him, Kornak "blows up" so to speak. First his head becomes larger (then much larger!) with that pointy beak full of gnarly teeth, very intimidating. The cops stop advancing. They're not sure what they are seeing. But it keeps happening. His body morphs to very large, and his clothes fly off ripped apart. Now, the police and the others are just terrified. He becomes so large that his head is hitting the ceiling as he thrashes around. The police stand frozen with fear, stunned. Jenkins and Tanya are hiding behind the counter. Kornak then lets out one of those screeches that's part of the act. You know the one—super scary!

So Kornak the hideous monster then pushes Officer Brooks out of his way and grabs all the leashes hanging on display. His big hands make it easy to get them all at once. He swings the leashes over to Adria and says, "Go!" She knows exactly what to do. She takes the leashes and shoots through the door that leads to the dogs. Out the second door and she is outside with the cages. Using her shape-shifting fingers, she goes down the row of cages opening the locks. She can hear the commotion inside where Kornak is keeping the others occupied as long as he can. And he's putting on a show too, screeching and knocking stuff around. At one point, he puts his hands in his armpits and crows like a rooster! He keeps them going for quite a little while. But when he turns to go out the same door as Adria, he knows it is too small for his big body. He has to squat down and turn his body sideways and just lunge through, causing damage to the doorframe.

The cops and the others aren't about to try to stop him from leaving! If he wants to leave without killing any of them, that would be good.

So Kornak busts through the second door like the first one—sideways, broken door frame, and all that. Now he's in the dog area where Adria has quite a few leashed up. She is at the far end of the fenced area, opening the fence gate. Kornak sees this going on, and he wants to catch up.

The people inside aren't offering any chase. They're still pretty dazed about what happened.

A couple looking to buy a dog walk in. The place is a mess, and four people are standing there with shocked looks on their faces. Officer Sapp greets them. Then he starts to mumble the story of what happened. "There was this kid . . . he got mad, and . . . well, he turned himself into a giant monster." He looks over at Brooks and asks, "Does that sound right?" Brooks just nods his head yes and says nothing. The couple can see that this is no joke. These four people are traumatized. So the couple decides quickly to leave and come back another day. Let these people get their act together.

Meanwhile outside, Adria has eight dogs on leashes. She also (in her haste) opened several cat cages. So there are cats running around too. They all take off across a field. They are heading toward the road that leads them home.

As Kornak (still in gigantic monster mode) has to squeeze through the fence gate and ruin it, he sees all the kennel doors open. He thinks, *Adria did a good job opening all those cages so fast! You go, girl!*

But anyway, he squeezes through the gate and takes off running too! And this monster can cover some ground fast. He looks kind of like an ostrich sprinting wide open, moving unbelievably fast. Big ole crazy-looking lizard thing cooking across a field!

He catches up with Adria and the dogs quickly. They all stop for a moment to check each other's well-being.

Adria (catching her breath) asks, "Are you okay, Kornak?"

Kornak answers, "Sure, just a little scratched up is all. Those doors are small. Let's get out of here!"

He reaches out and picks up Adria with one arm and as many dogs as he can carry in the other. Adria seems surprised at first, but then sees the sense in it. This guy can move fast!

Once everyone is loaded on his arms and shoulders, Adria and six dogs, Kornak takes off running again! Two dogs are following trying to keep up. Leashes are dragging. Cats are running too! It's a jailbreak!

By now, the people inside the dog pound are coming out of shock. Jenkins and Tanya are tidying up a bit. A lot of debris lying around. The cops cautiously, with guns drawn, follow the route that thing took, through busted doors. Both officers are nervous as hell. Whatever it was sure looked like it could kill someone pretty easy. It's so unbelievable.

Back out in the field, Kornak stops to rest a second and to let the other two dogs catch up. He is carrying his load well and got 'em all balanced just right.

As they approach the road, there's a lot of traffic. People can see this thing (at least the ones who are looking that way can see him). What a sight—an unidentified creature, body obscured by dogs and one person. It's running superfast. If you blink, you'd miss it!

Adria cautions Kornak to watch out for these cars. She's thinking he's going to stop and wait for a break in the traffic to cross. Bullcrap! He hurdles both lanes of traffic easily. He is like an Olympic hurdler. People in their cars who saw it are in awe! It's hard for your brain to process something so crazy looking. He lands perfectly, still in full stride, and doesn't miss a lick.

Adria goes from being scared to having fun. She's still holding on for life, but there's a smile on her face!

As Officer Brooks gets to the ruined fence gate at the far end of the kennels, he holsters his pistol. He can see Kornak and his group in the distance, just as he makes his hurdle. Brooks looks down and just shakes his head. *What was that?* he thinks. *What the hell was that?!*

Kornak and his cargo don't have very far to go before they get to the ship, about a quarter mile. He sprints past where they had played football and approaches the field where the ship is hidden.

Now the police officers have gathered their composure, and they are getting into their car to offer some kind of pursuit. Luckily their car wasn't damaged in the may-lay that occurred inside. They both are still pretty dazed. But they have a job to do. As we know, cops don't scare easy, but man that was crazy!

Out on the road, where the traffic is heavy, two dogs are trying to cross. They want to rejoin their friends who have already crossed. But bless their hearts. Dogs aren't very good at crossing busy roads. Both are fairly large dogs, one brown lab mix and the other looking like a hound. Both of their new leashes are dragging the ground. Adria meant well when she put the leashes on them, but now the dogs are tripping over them.

The brown dog makes his break, running in front of a guy in a Volvo. Luckily the guy sees him coming and slams on his brakes. The Volvo hits the dog but only slightly. There's a loud sound of brakes squealing and a dog yelping loudly, followed by the sound of a crash. The guy behind the Volvo couldn't stop in time. So now there's a wreck. It helps the second dog get across the road. Whew!

Kornak has just now made it to the camouflage ring, when he hears the sounds back a ways up the road. He looks back that way worried. He heard the dog yelp. So Kornak (still in monster mode) quickly puts Adria and the dogs down and tells her he will be right back. He shoots back out of the cover of woods to go help. He didn't really notice two hippie-looking dudes sleeping in their stuck car. As he gets back to the road, he sees the two dogs, apparently okay and running toward him. They look happy as can be! The hound dog is barking!

Kornak scoops them up with his long arms and holds them against his chest, like they're a couple of Chihuahuas or something! As he looks up the road where the wreck happened, he sees red and blue lights back a little ways farther. He's not sure what that means. He thinks, *Red and blue lights, huh.*

It's the police, the same two who just left the dog pound, Brooks and Sapp. Only now they're stuck in a traffic jam that the doggies caused. Both cops are still kind of dazed, having seen what they've seen.

So they have to pull onto the shoulder to get up there and see what's going on. It most surely has something to do with that thing they encountered at the pound.

On board the ship, Zilog is worried. He's also impatient. He wants his people back, hopefully unharmed. He's pacing, somewhat calmly outside the ship. He's holding Lucy, so that helps. There are no passengers outside today. Zilog wants to be ready to go when the "gold shipment" arrives. So all the passengers are safe inside.

He sees someone coming through the woods. At first, he doesn't know who it is. Then he hears the sound of dogs grunting and whining. So he's pretty sure it's Kornak and Adria. He breathes a sigh of relief, knowing that one of his crews has returned safely. But it's only Adria.

Zilog sees her and six more dogs come into the clearing. She's very happy to see him, happy to be home! Zilog asks her, "Where's Kornak?" He almost doesn't want to hear it if it's bad news.

He thinks back to when he was so angry with him that he hoped Kornak would get captured or killed. Now he feels terrible for thinking that.

But Adria answers cheerfully, "Oh, he's coming, sir. We had a couple of stragglers, so he went back for them." Zilog is so relieved when he heard that! Adria goes on, "Everything is fine, sir. We got some more dogs!" She didn't say anything about the big scene at the dog pound or the police being there. She'll get to all that. Right now, she just wants to assure her commander that everything is okay. He'll get to hear about Kornak morphing into a badass monster and saving the situation.

Then all of a sudden, Zilog's hand starts buzzing! He had knelt down to meet the new dogs and pet them and such. But now he stands back up (still holding Lucy) and raises his hand to his face.

He talks to his hand, "Blue to red, receiving your transmission."

Mezruh answers, "Hello, sir! We have good news!"

"That's great! Let me in on it!"

"We have gold, sir!" He's almost yelling with excitement! "We have more than enough to get us home!"

"That's marvelous! And when can I expect your arrival?"

"Well, sir, we're in the air, flying parallel to the highway. So I'm watching for you and the ship. It shouldn't be long."

Zilog replies, relieved, "Sounds great, Mezruh. Just get here as soon as you can."

"Orders received, sir!" He's so excited you can hear it in his voice.

Just then, the truck goes zooming by behind Zilog! The loud noise of the power booster startles him as it roars by! He looks over his shoulder in time to see the bottom of the truck with the booster on it. So he knows it's them. Who else would it be?

He quickly pulls his hand to his face and says loudly, "You just passed us, Mezruh! You passed us! Turn that rig around!" He's sort of laughing as he talks. Zilog has so much confidence in his boys that he can take this lightly. He knows they are almost home.

Mezruh responds, "I see you now, sir!" He says loudly, "I'll get her turned back around!"

Meanwhile, here come the choppers! They want to know what's going on here. What's up with this rocket-powered flying truck? Whose crazy invention is this? It looks pretty impressive zooming by, a flying truck! What the f——!

Meantime, in the truck, Mezruh uses his control knobs (one that steers whatever the booster is attached to), and he makes a wide arc in the sky. Now they're headed in the right direction. It takes a few minutes to right the ship.

The cops are now at the accident scene, taking statements from all involved. When the truck roared by the first time, it sure got everyone's attention. And as people at the scene go back to discussing the accident, they see the flying truck go far away in the sky and begin to circle back, very distracting to the people trying to talk about this accident.

Kornak has made it to the ship with the two dogs he went back for. But this time, he does notice the two guys and their car stuck in the muddy field. But Kornak has bigger things to do. He thinks to himself, *I've got to let my commander know I'm back from my mission, and then I'll go and help those guys, who ever they are.*

Zilog is outside the ship, watching the Chevy truck make a circle in the sky. And, yes, he's holding Lucy. Kornak and his two dogs come up behind Zilog. Kornak puts his dogs down and pats his commander on the shoulder. Zilog turns to see who patted him and is thoroughly startled to see Kornak in monster form. At first Zilog didn't recognize him. Lucy barks at him.

Zilog exclaims, "Geeze! You scared the holy crap out of me! Is that you, Kornak?"

"Yes, sir. Sorry to startle you. I'll explain, sir, but right now that truck is almost here."

Kornak can see that Zilog is very intent on watching the truck land (or whatever it's going to do).

So he takes his two dogs, and he heads back around to the other side of the ship where Tom and Jerry are stuck in the mud. Kornak realizes that he is still in giant lizard form, and he may scare them at first. But he'll need this big form to get that car unstuck. It looked like it was stuck pretty bad.

Tom and Jerry had been sleeping in their car. They dug for a while last night but couldn't get the car out, so they had fallen asleep on the seats, until the rocket truck went by. And the two choppers also make a ton of noise. It's definitely time for Tom and Jerry to be getting up.

So they come dragging ass out of the car, stretching, yawning, and wondering what all the noise is about. Then they go back to their grim work of getting their car out of this damn mud.

They were asleep when Adria ran by with her dogs. Then they were both looking down when Kornak ran by carrying two big dogs. Both Tom and Jerry are digging and wedging plywood under the back wheels. They haven't seen the rocket truck flying around yet or the big monster that's coming to help them.

And here he comes now! Kornak steps out of the woods, with his dogs, and gets right behind Tom and Jerry without them realizing it. There's a lot of noise from the choppers, and they are both looking down at their situation. Kornak asks them, talking loudly over the choppers, "You guys need some help?" he says casually. Both Tom and Jerry look up at the same time to see this giant lizard-looking thing (with two dogs on leashes). So Tom and Jerry both freak out at seeing this, of course. They both scramble to their feet and hurry to the far end of the car, scared to death! Both are screaming hysterically as Kornak tries to calm them down. He tells them, "I'm here to help you." Tom and Jerry are still hysterical. But they're about done screaming. Kornak goes on, "I came to help I said!" He points at the sky and goes on, "Do you see that truck coming?" Tom and Jerry both look where he is pointing and see the flying truck coming straight at them from the sky, another reason to freak out! Kornak goes on, "We've got to get your car out of here, so that truck can come in, right about here where your car is! So stop screaming and let's do this!" He then starts picking up their stuff that's lying on the ground and putting it in the trunk—the shovels and the scissor jack. "Do you guys want this?" he says holding up the muddy plywood. Both Tom and Jerry nod their heads yes, although both are still dazed about all this. So Kornak chucks the plywood into the trunk. He looks like he's getting impatient. "You guys get in," he says as he slams the trunk. The dogs start barking when the trunk slams. Tom and Jerry scurry into the car as Kornak takes a hold of the back bumper with one hand. Tom starts the engine even though his hands are trembling. He slams on the gas as Kornak lifts the car way up out of the mud. The power wheel is spinning fast as Kornak pushes the car out of the rut it was in. So she's unstuck! Tom keeps the gas on until he's surely out of stuckville. (It's a word. Look it up, okay maybe not.) Anyway, Tom gets it out of the path of the truck that's coming in for a landing. He sees in his mirror Kornak and his dogs go back into the woods they came out of. Tom and Jerry can't believe what just happened or that there's a flying truck coming! It's all happening so fast! But they are sticking around to see what's gonna happen with that truck. It's coming in for what looks like will be a rough landing. Tom does a U-turn so they can watch better, like at the drive-in.

And here comes the truck! Mezruh has the booster all the way down. He's looking to coast in smoothly. See how that goes.

So now Zilog, Adria, Kornak, and eight dogs are the welcoming committee. But Tom and Jerry are watching too. They don't want to miss this! Mezruh and Orsello are the triumphant warriors, returning home with the ingredient they went out for. The plan seems to be coming together.

At the accident up the road a little, people are standing around looking to the sky. No one is talking. They're watching the flying truck.

And the policemen, Sapp and Brooks, decide to leave this accident scene and go see where that truck is going to land. Sapp says to Brooks, "What a crazy day this is turning into!"

Brooks nods yes and says, "Isn't it though?" He pulls the car on down to the field where the truck is coming in for a landing. The policemen get out of their car and stand behind their doors, watching intently!

"Trucks just don't fly," Brooks says loudly! Tom and Jerry are sitting in their car watching too. They are still kind of in shock.

Both choppers are circling the area. They still want to know what's going on here!

"This is Channel 6 Action News, reporting live from the news chopper," the lady reporter says. "We've got a crazy scene going on here today! It seems as though an inventor has a device on a truck that makes it fly."

Other cars are stopping and slowing down. People have never seen anything like this before!

Onboard the truck, Mezruh is controlling it as best he can. He's got the booster setting as low as it goes, but they're still going pretty fast. He doesn't dare turn it off. They would drop like a rock. They don't want that.

Orsello puts his big green head in the busted-out window and gives Mezruh moral support. He says, "We've been through some rough landings before, bro! We can do this. It'll be fun you'll see."

Mezruh looks over at him and says with anger, "Fun? Fun you say?"

Big O says, "Yeah! Let's get bouncy!"

Mezruh says, "I'm morphing big like you. Those big bodies can take more impact than these skinny little human bodies." He then grips the steering wheel and makes a mad face. His body grows instantly, and he sticks his head out the window.

With his body exploding into a huge one, he can't fit in the cab anymore. So he's hanging out the driver's window not looking very comfortable at all. Then he pops the door open from the outside handle. As the door opens, Mezruh is reaching back inside to get as much gold off the seat as he can. He's holding it against his body like a wad of dirty laundry. Orsello sees him doing this and starts to gather all the gold items he has in the back of the truck. Mezruh, now in a full-blown monster form, is hanging out the door of the truck. His hands and arms are full of gold items, McDonald's bags and ketchup packs. Orsello has all his stuff gathered too, including something he didn't realize he grabbed. It's a wrestler's championship belt, big gaudy-looking thing hanging over his shoulder. He's the champ!

As the truck gets closer to the ground, they get ready to jump off. They have quite an audience too. People watch from their cars, the police are there, and Tom and Jerry aren't going anywhere.

All watch intently as the truck comes in. What a crazy sight—a pickup truck flying. Like that's not enough, it's got two monstrosities hanging off of it, covered with what looks like bling!

When the truck is about twenty feet above the ground, but still moving pretty fast, Mezruh jumps, no fear. Orsello is also fearless, and he jumps too, gold flying everywhere! The witnesses are getting a show! They'll have a wild story to tell at the dinner table tonight!

Back in the news chopper, the lady reporter is reporting stuff that doesn't sound real.

Let's listen in: "And now it looks as though these two dinosaurs are jumping out. Both have their hands full of something, gold maybe? I've never seen anything like this!"

As Mezruh and Orsello hit the ground, they tumble hard, like someone who had jumped off a speeding train, rough landing. Both lose a lot of their gold all over the ground. They frantically pick up as much as they can see. They (and everyone else) see the truck crash to the ground and tumble over and over.

By now, Zilog has returned to the control room and has started the combustion blowers.

He is readying the ship for takeoff. He also pushes the button that deactivates the camouflage around the ship. This causes even more amazement to the onlookers! Suddenly where there was a large patch of woods, there is now a huge spaceship! Tom and Jerry are so stunned at this that they both just sit there frozen. They wonder what the hell they are looking at.

And Kornak was right about where the truck would land. It wound up laying right where Tom and Jerry's car had been stuck. Good call, Kornak!

So he and Adria rush to help their comrades gather gold from the ground. And with them come their dogs, barking playfully. Mezruh and Orsello can't believe it! "Dogs?!" Mezruh yells. "You guys got dogs?!" He drops to one knee and puts his gold down as the dogs run up to him.

Orsello sees this as inappropriate and yells sternly at his buddy, "What are you doing, Mezruh? Pet the dogs later! We've got to get this gold in the ship!" Adria and Kornak are helping hurry things up, gathering gold and restraining the dogs. Mezruh gets up, having regained his composure. He picks up his gold, and they all move very quickly (gold, dogs, and all) to the ship.

Up the cargo ramp they go. Zilog is waiting at the control panel for the door. He closes the door quickly as everyone gets inside.

The choppers are still hovering about, their occupants staring and mumbling about what just happened. Even the reporter gal is so stunned that she's not talking at all, just staring. The policemen and all the other witnesses who stopped to watch, why they're all shocked too. All are just standing there, with their mouths open— shocked and in awe! Not only was there a flying truck that crashed into the field, but crazy-looking lizard men jumped out! And to top that off, they all ran into a huge spaceship! And there were dogs too! Where do they fit in? Who knows?! The people of this small town are getting quite a show. Extraterrestrials don't come around here too often (never).

Now, onboard the ship, Zilog is in control of the takeoff. He puts the combustion blowers on high rpm, which creates a huge dust cloud outside. People are forced to get back in their cars. The choppers are forced to up to a higher altitude to avoid the blinding dust.

Then, inside the ship, Mezruh has an urgent request. He asks Zilog, "Commander, do you think we should retrieve the power booster? We don't want this race to have our advanced technology."

Zilog thinks for a long second and agrees. After all, the beings here haven't really mounted any attack on them. So it seems relatively safe. He slows the rpm on the blowers to idle speed. He then turns to Mezruh and says very seriously, "Go get it."

Now Mezruh jumps into action. He runs down the corridor to the cargo bay. He pushes the down button, and out into the dust-filled atmosphere he goes, still looking like a dinosaur with gym shorts on.

At first he can't see very well because of all the dust the blowers made. Once he gets his bearings, he can see the truck (wrecked and crumpled) that was his home the last two days.

It's lying upside down. The power booster looks okay though, not bent or damaged. It is hot though, hot as balls! But that doesn't deter Mezruh from his task of removing it. *Ow, ow, owie! This thing is hot!* he thinks to himself as he pulls it off. Soon he has it off, cables and all. As he is getting the knob assembly, he looks over and he sees their beloved radio. So he grabs it too and yanks it right out of the dash, wires hanging off and all. So he's got the radio, and he picks up the power booster which is still hot! So he drops it and picks it up by the cables and drags it. He hurries back to the cargo ramp with his load. Nobody outside can see him through the dusty air so he makes it safely. Up and inside he goes. Zilog and Adria are waiting for him at the control panel. They're happy to see he's okay! Zilog closes the door as soon as Mezruh gets in. Zilog proclaims, "Okay! Now let's get out of here!"

They all hurry up the corridor to the bridge. Mezruh morphs back to normal size and shape (lizard-like but not big and scary). As Zilog and Adria return to the bridge, Mezruh goes to his quarters for some clothes. Kornak and Orsello have also morphed back to normal too. The big bodies did their job. Now it's time to go.

Zilog takes his seat and again brings the combustion blowers back up to full rpm. And here goes the huge dust cloud outside again.

In the work area of the propulsion room, Orsello, Mezruh, and Kornak have gathered to sort the gold to be processed into liquid and then to vapor. The gold is piled on the work table mixed with sod and McDonald's wrappers and bags and some ketchup packets. It looks like a pile of garbage. There's a smashed-up Reese's peanut butter cup and a bag of jerky mixed in. But once sorted and cleaned, the gold will make fine fuel for their ship.

Meanwhile, Zilog has the motors at full rpm. The huge saucer begins to raise up into the sky amid even more dust. People are in awe more than ever, watching this thing going straight up.

What a sight, to be watching a UFO taking off—and a huge one at that! It's an awesome but scary thing to witness.

And of course, there's a coverup. On the news that evening, a military guy says that all this UFO stuff is false. He assures everyone that what they all saw was a weather balloon, nothing more. It's just a weather balloon. He has no comment about the truck flying through the sky that everyone saw. "You're all seeing things! It was just a weather balloon, a new military experiment. Yeah, that's it!" he says. It's a typical explanation from military brass. "You're all nuts. It was just a balloon."

On board the ship, the mood is jovial! Everyone is relieved and happy. Zilog has the ship high in the atmosphere, so high up that to the people on the ground, it looks like a speck. Then it's gone, into Earth's outer atmosphere. Nothing is left to see except a wrecked pickup truck and a big hole in the ground where the ship took off.

Later in the evening, the crowd has all gone home. Everyone who witnessed any of this can't stop talking about it with those who missed it. The whole town is abuzz with it. The dog pound is a mess. The gold outlet store (in another town) is a big mess. The armored car company is out forty grand. But by God, people sure have something to talk about!

And onboard the V-34, people have something to talk about too. This has been quite an unexpected adventure for them. Even though none of the passengers got to mingle with the humans, it was still exciting. And they have dogs! Yes, they do—dogs to take to the new planet! What a joyful miracle for people who have missed them for so long. Never again will dogs be eliminated from their lives.

And Mezruh and Orsello are anxious to share their new discovery with everyone—rock n' roll!

They get the radio wired into the ship's intercom system. But reception is lousy as they get farther away from Earth. But luckily, there's a CD in it that the boys didn't even know about.

And what is it? Why classic rock, of course! Mezruh takes the disc out and examines it. He looks at Orsello and giggles saying, "Look at this Earth technology here."

Orsello tells him, "Put it back in. Let's see what happens."

So Mezruh puts the CD back on the little tray. It goes in by itself. They look at each other and smile. And suddenly rock music comes on! It's AC/DC! T.N.T.

See me ride out of the sunset on your color TV screen. I'm for all that I can get, if you know what I mean.

And it's playing on the intercom system throughout the ship! Passengers and crew aren't sure if they like it at first. But the music becomes more enjoyable the more they listen. Mezruh and Orsello start dancing erratically with the music. Arms are flailing wildly and bodies bouncing in beat with the music. It's a funny sight!

Kornak laughs at this amusement. He's never known these two to have a lighter side, probably because of the stressful situation they were in. But seeing them dancing all crazy is just so funny! So Kornak starts dancing to it a little too. He's not into it as much as they are, but he's moving a little. Rock will do that to you.

This seems like a nice way to end our story—the ship jetting off into the cosmos. If it were a movie, this is where the credits would start to roll. People are getting up to leave the theatre. But wait! On screen Mezruh comes up from behind the credits and tears them down, holding the wrinkled mess against his chest as he yells at the audience, "Don't leave yet, you guys! There's more!" He seems very excited, not wanting the story to be over. He is standing in the cargo bay as he motions us to follow him. Still holding all the credits in a crumpled mess, he turns and hurries out the door and up the corridor toward the ship's helm.

With buzzer-style alarms going off through the ship, Mezruh (in his original lizard-like appearance) hurries through the corridor, stopping to put the movie credits in a trash can.

He looks back to see if we moviegoers are still following. We are.

Mezruh then rushes into the main control room and the helm if you will, where red lights are flashing and buzzers are sounding. Something is wrong! Zilog is seated in his commander's chair, looking very concerned.

The ship is flying well. The new fuel made from gold is performing like it should.

The problem is approaching obstacles in space—a meteor shower, a dreaded meteor shower!

It's like the ones that killed Zilog's friends. He looks nervous and angry at the same time. The other crewmembers are present also, and all agree that the situation is dire!

On one computer monitor that resembles a radar screen, the menacing meteors can be seen approaching their ship at eleven o'clock, coming right at them! Zilog knows that this ship has much improved acceleration although until now he hasn't used it or needed to. But now it's time to see how good it works! He instructs all present to strap in. They obey his order. All crewmembers are in stationary chairs with seatbelts of course. The chairs flip up out of the floor hydraulically. Pretty cool.

But those alarms going off aren't to cool. Zilog hits the acknowledge button that silences the alarms. He's aware of the situation, so he doesn't need the blaring alarms any more. They're killing everyone's ears!

Zilog knows he cannot fly into this mess and try to dodge meteors as he goes! *I'm not doing that,* he thinks to himself. *That's how you get yourself killed!* So he decides to use another method. Retreat. Yes, he's using precious fuel, but he must do it. He can't ponder his options for long. He has to act now. He tells his crew what his intentions are, reversing their course, and proceeds to slow the ship. As the ship comes to a slow rate of speed, Zilog is able to turn the craft around carefully (skillfully) while still monitoring the meteors on the radar. The other crewmembers marvel proudly at their commander's competency in this dangerous situation. Adria thinks, *He sure can fly this big thing.*

Once he has the ship turned around, it's only a matter of outrunning the enemy. And, yes, the V-34 has much improved acceleration. (Did I mention that?) The ship zooms like a stallion through space, back toward Earth. They easily outrun the meteor shower.

When they are safely away from the meteors, Zilog slows the craft down to idle speed. He needs to reverse his course to get back on track to their destination. With this done, his course is set, on to the new planet! The meteors are gone.

The V-34 zooms past the international space station, causing a big ripple in those guys' day.

It flipped the whole thing upside down! The astronauts didn't get much of a look at the big bad V-34 as it streaked by them. But they'll be okay. There's no gravity in there anyway. Stuff's always floating around.

Okay, let's get back to our heroes. They are all unbuckling from their restraints and beginning to move about. The crew and commander are all back in their original reptilian appearance.

Their crazy episode with the humans is over. They just needed to stop in for some fuel.

The conversation is light as people move to their workstations. The safety seats flip back into the floor. (Nifty!) Everyone knew Zilog would perform in an excellent manner, calmly maneuvering them from a deadly situation.

From this point, the voyage will take a little more time to complete. They're about halfway there. All three of the fuel tanks are looking good. The gold they brought on board (made off with) was melted and vaporized with no problem. The tank is about three quarters full. The V-34 is the first ship to have this equipment. It was crucial!

So now they're zooming along. Everything is going well. The passengers are gathered in the rec area. Some are chatting and visiting with each other, while others are jamming to the rock music coming through the intercom system. The song playing is by the Beatles, "Paperback writer."

Dear sirs or madams, will you read my book? It took me years to write. Will you take a look? It's based on a novel by a man named Lear and I need a job, so I want to be a paperback writer.

Some of the passengers are dancing to it—cool scene.

Then someone comes up with the idea to ask Zilog to shoot some of that calming mist their way. They remember how it made them feel the last time they experienced it. It felt good! So some people who aren't dancing and rocking out go up to the camera monitor. They start chanting softly, "Calming mist, calming mist." They aren't trying to sound mean or mutinous (is that a word?), but gently requesting some of that calming mist. Is that asking so much? Besides, the dogs are getting rowdy. Yeah, that's it! It's for the dogs.

In his seat at the helm, Zilog can see what's going on. He's in a good mood. He's got Lucy on his lap. So he concedes to their request and hits the button to "calm" everyone. But he inadvertently leaves it going throughout the ship, instead of just the rec area.

So pretty soon the whole house is mellow. Even the dogs are calm! Also, the crew flying the ship has calmed down. Not so much that they can't do their jobs, just in a mellower state. That's all.

It's sort of like someone who has been smoking pot.

The passengers in the rec area go into a cheer when they see the mist coming through the vents. Now it's really party time! Someone says loudly, "Commander Zilog comes through for us again! He's the man!" From his seat Zilog just smiles. What a great feeling for him, knowing they had come through so much adversity. And now all are safe and on their way. At this moment, he loves his job. And he knows for sure that his passengers are so going to love their new planet. That's in the bag. He's going to see some happy faces that day for sure! Zilog has seen these amazed happy looks before, on all his previous runs. Happy, happy, joy, joy! Okay, I stole that from *The Ren and Stimpy Show*. But yeah, he's seen some joy as people departed his ship upon landing on H-2.

Zilog looks up to his monitor of the rec area, and he sees that everyone there is dancing to rock music, Aerosmith's "Train Kept a Rolling." Zilog smiles gently and goes back to flying his ship.

As they get closer to their new home, Zilog finally makes radio contact with his superiors on H-2. At first their signals are garbled, but Zilog can tell he's reached his people. *What a relief,* he thinks, *to finally talk to someone.* So he establishes himself as the commander of the V-34. The home base operator, called air traffic control here on Earth, can't believe his ears! They had given up on the V-34 for dead. A normal voyage would have had them there three days ago.

There is utter jubilance among the control center! The others can't believe it either! All on the new planet had begun grieving the loss of this ship and its beloved passengers. But NO, they are alive and on their way home! Woo-hoo!

Zilog didn't mention in his communication that they had acquired dogs. He thought he would save that surprise for when they arrived and lowered the cargo bay door. *What a surprise this will be,* he thinks to himself. He's bringing them the miracle of dogs! It will blow them away!

And so, the remainder of the trip is smooth. There's no fuel shortage, no more meteor showers, and no landing on some strange hostile planet.

The "V-base" as it is called on H-2 resembles an airport, a large building in the center with corridor-style hallways that lead out to the ships. Can you picture it? It's like an airport. Only the ships are round, not airplane style.

It's a busy place. People (reptilian-looking people) move about as the ships unload. The ship's primary missions are to shuttle people here from Nibiru. So the atmosphere here is almost always jovial. People exit their craft literally stunned by the beauty of their new home. Wouldn't you be?

So here comes the V-34. And all her crew and passengers are alive and well! A small crowd is gathering as the ship sets down. People are amazed that this ship is even here. It had been presumed lost. It was for a while.

Inside the ship, Zilog shuts down the blowers, as all prepare to disembark. This is it! The passengers are assembling in the cargo area. The party is over. It's time to leave. All are mellow from the . . . you know what.

Zilog assembles his crew proudly at the cargo bay door. Each of them has one of the larger dogs on a leash, except Zilog who is carrying his Lucy. Mezruh pushes the open button and turns to the other crewmembers with a smile on his reptilian face.

As the cargo door opens down, all the crowd that has gathered to greet them are amazed to see that Zilog and his crew have brought them dogs! All are ecstatic. They can't believe it!

It's a true miracle. The crowd goes wild!

Adria knew all this would happen. She had pictured all this in her mind. And she made all of this come true. She couldn't have done it without Kornak and Zilog. But by being persistent, she made it happen!

As the crew walk down the ramp with their dogs, they mingle into the loving crowd. And the passengers come down the ramp too. Some are with more dogs. One person even has a kitty cat. It's a beautiful scene.

I think that's the end, for now, although there are many possible ways for this story to continue! Stay tuned.

ABOUT THE AUTHOR

TIMOTHY NEWBREY IS A SIXTY-YEAR-OLD retired factory worker or equipment operator. He was born in Utica, New York, but made his home in Tampa, Florida.

He graduated from Robinson High School and spent twenty years at a gypsum company in Port Tampa (wallboard manufacturing).

In writing this story, Tim used some of his favorite things in combination: his love for dogs, football, rock 'n' roll, and the study of life on other planets, UFOs, and such—all mixed together for one crazy story.

Tim, also known as Joe, his middle name, is married to his wife, Sara. They have two grown kids and three tiny grandkids.